A Soldier's Pledge

Beyond Valor 5

An Eagle Security & Protection Agency Novel

Lynne St. James

A Soldier's Pledge

Copyright © 2017 by Lynne St. James
Cover Art Copyright © 2017 by Lynne St. James
Published by Coffee Bean Press
Cover Art Design by LoriJacksonDesign.com
Created in the United States

This book is a work of fiction. Names, characters, places, and incidents are products of the author's imagination or used fictitiously. Any resemblance to actual events or locales or persons living or dead is entirely coincidental.

No part of this work may be used, stored, reproduced or transmitted without written permission from the publisher except for brief quotations for review purposes as permitted by law.

This book is licensed for your personal enjoyment only and may not be re-sold or given away to other people. If you would like to share this book, please purchase an additional copy for each person.

If you're reading this book and did not purchase it, or it was not purchased for your use, please purchase your own copy. Thank you for respecting the hard work of this author.

A Soldier's Pledge

He'd do anything to keep her safe.
Ethan Price thought a job as a small-town police detective in Willow Haven would be easy after five years as a pilot in the Air Force. Then a rash of break-ins put the entire department on alert and the woman he loves at risk.

Too stubborn for her own good.
Anna Taggart is smart, stubborn, independent, and doesn't think she needs anyone. Having her heart broken before, she refuses to give in to her feelings for Ethan no matter how hard he pursues her.

Can he get through to her before it's too late?
When the clues lead to someone close to Anna, Ethan has his work cut out for him. With help from his partner, Steele, and the team at Eagle Security & Protection he is determined to solve the case and keep Anna safe. But will Ethan be able to convince Anna that life is too short not to give in to love?

DEDICATION

For T.S. my hero!

ACKNOWLEDGMENTS

Thank you to the #coffeecrew and #wordwarriors for their daily support and smiles. Thank you too, to Caitlyn O'Leary. For all the phone calls, sprinting, and whip cracking that we do to keep each other on track, I am forever grateful.

CHAPTER ONE

Anna Taggart parked her car in front of 3232 Seashell Lane and double checked her paperwork. Double checking was her thing, maybe it was her undiagnosed OCD or just her, she never knew. Not that it mattered. She always had to check and cross check for as long as she could remember.

The house was cute, in an old-timey Florida way. A typical pink seashell stucco bungalow with bright yellow hibiscus plants blooming in the front yard. Anna couldn't have asked for a more perfect setting for an open house. Now she just had to hope that the inside looked as good as the outside. If it did, she might be able to sell it today. She didn't get a chance to make many sales anymore so this could be fun. At least, that's what she kept telling herself.

First, she had to make sure the house was clean, a comfortable temperature, and smelled great. It was one of the most important parts of the open house and was one of the first things she shared with her new real estate agents when they came on board. That and the trick about baking cookies. There was nothing more tempting to anyone who walked into the house than the smell of cookies fresh out of the oven.

As CEO of Willow Haven Realty, Anna didn't usually spend her Saturdays holding open houses. Instead, you could usually find her at her desk dealing with the mounds of paperwork that multiplied faster than bunnies. The paperwork would still be there tomorrow and helping her best friend was more than worth a few extra hours of work on a Sunday. When she'd scheduled the open house, Adria had no idea her son's soccer team would make the finals, or that the game would be today. The best solution had been for Anna to help, this way if it sold Adria would still get the commission, rather than have another agent take it over.

Thinking back to when she met Adria for the first time still made her smile. She'd come into the office just before closing on a Tuesday evening. No experience, tons of enthusiasm, and a great personality all convinced Anna to give her a chance. It wasn't until a few months later that she had learned Adria's husband had been shot down over Iraq. It was crazy that it was four years already. Anna had been happy to hire her, but Adria had become her best friend, something Anna hadn't had in a very long time. That alone was worth giving up a hundred Saturdays.

Grabbing her "go-bag" as she liked to call it and an open house sign from her back seat, she got out of the car mumbling a prayer as she climbed up the stoop to the front door. With about an hour to spare, she should have just enough time to make sure the house was clean, pop a batch of cookies in the oven and put out the fresh flowers and candles she had in her bag.

With a whispered prayer that the house was in good shape, she unlocked the lockbox, opened the front door and stopped inside. The realtor gods were smiling down on her for sure, and she would have done a fist pump if her hands weren't full. Not only was it clean, but it was also adorable and the perfect house for snowbirds or a young family. Adria had said the sellers were anxious because they'd been transferred overseas, and if her luck held she might be able to sell it today.

After a quick walk-through, Anna put the cookies in the oven and set up staging the house. By the time the buzzer sounded, she had candles lit, soft music playing, the dining room table set, and the flowers in vases. Once the cookies were cool, she'd put the platter on the dining room table to entice her 'guests' as they came through the door. Her company wasn't the number one realty in Willow Haven for no reason. Even though it was a small town, she had competition from the large realtor chains.

One more quick check through the house and Anna was satisfied. It was time for the last step, putting the sign in the front yard. Grabbing the balloons she'd brought to attach to the sign, she opened the front door, stepped outside, and collided with a rock-hard t-shirt-clad chest. Backing away on instinct alone, it took her brain a moment to register that she knew that chest. Very well, in fact.

"Hi, sweetheart."

"Damn it, Ethan. You scared the crap out of me."

"It wasn't intentional, but I didn't expect you to open the door as I was about to knock." He might be saying he was sorry, but his smart-ass grin said otherwise. And oh, how she loved that smile and the way his eyes crinkled at the corners, and the dimple that appeared on his right cheek. *Stop it. Get a grip, girl.* She knew better.

"How did you know I was here?" Every last inch of his six-foot three-inch frame was good enough to eat, and she'd tasted just about all of it. Sex with Ethan was beyond amazing, and just thinking about it make her hot and bothered. But now wasn't the time or the place. Staring at this bulging biceps and ripped abdomen outlined by his t-shirt, wouldn't do her a damn bit of good.

"I stopped by the office. Jenny said you were covering Adria's open house. Don't you have enough on your plate already?"

"It's not a big deal. Besides, you know Adria would do anything for me. Scotty's soccer team made the finals. I thought I told you last night?"

Ethan Price, ex-Air Force pilot and Willow Haven police detective, rolled his eyes and shook his head. It wasn't the first time he'd given her that look. And it wasn't like she hadn't made it clear from the beginning that friends with benefits was all she could handle. But he made it clear that he wanted more, a lot more, every chance he got. "You run yourself ragged."

"It's my company."

"No, it's your father's company. He just lets you do all the work." He was right even if she didn't want to admit it. Her parents had retired four years earlier and left her to run the business while they hit every golf course in the world.

"That's not entirely true."

"C'mon, it's true, and you know it."

With a sigh, she pushed past him to set up the sign. It was an old argument, one they'd been having for months. She knew he admired how she worked hard and took care of all her employees or 'work family' as she usually called them. But he didn't like that she worked twenty-four/seven, and didn't or wouldn't take more time for herself.

It would be easy to give in, to commit more of herself to their relationship. Much too easy. And that was the problem. She didn't want to get hurt again, didn't want to have to put together the shattered pieces of her broken heart. Losing Ryan had devastated her, she'd barely been able to get out of bed and face the world. Then a few months later Brad or as he liked everyone to call him now, Tag, was almost killed, she threw herself into work. It was that or lose it totally. Too much pain, too much loss. Work was easier.

"Why are you here, anyway? Ugh. Sorry, that sounded kind of harsh. I thought you had to work today." He'd turned around to face her as she put the sign in the front yard. Every inch of his frame oozed sexy as he leaned against the doorway.

"Nope, this is my weekend off. Which is why I figured we could sneak in a little afternoon fun. Or I did until I realized you weren't in the office."

"Oh, you did, huh? What makes you think I'd have time for some afternoon nookie?"

"Hmm. I think I'd have found a way to convince you."

Seeing the gleam in his steel-blue eyes sent a shiver of desire down her spine. Damn. She'd tried so hard to keep him at arm's length, but he was just too—everything. Everything she wanted, everything she needed, and everything she was terrified of having again. Why was she even thinking about this now? She had an open house to run and stacks of paperwork waiting back at the office. Maybe it was time to put some distance between them, it was getting too hard to say no to him.

His quick smile proved he knew how he affected her. "I brought lunch. We both know you never remember to eat, and I figured since I couldn't have you, we could at least have lunch together. You have to eat."

Unable to resist his smile, she grinned. "Oh well. You win some, you lose some."

"I consider this a win. I still get to spend time with you."

"I don't have a lot of time. Buyers could show up any minute, and it's not professional to be eating on the job."

"Then I guess you'll have to eat fast. Jenny said you'd have time."

"Good thing I don't employ Jenny to keep secrets."

"She can't resist my charm."

Snorting, Anna shook her head. "Yeah, I'm sure that's exactly why."

"Hey, if you don't want what I've brought…"

"What did you bring?" She couldn't see the writing on the bag, but from his huge grin, she'd bet anything he'd gone to the best sandwich place in Willow Haven. If he had, he was right. She wouldn't be able to resist.

"I stopped at Dixie's. You know you can't turn down one of her roast beef sandwiches."

"That's so not fair!" Her mouth watered just thinking about the thin-sliced rare roast beef, provolone, and fresh tomatoes from Dixie's garden. All placed with extra care on top of two slices of the homemade sour dough bread she'd have made that morning. Dixie's food was like a little slice of heaven.

"Why not? I promise I won't tell the boss." Anna laughed. She couldn't help it. His eyes sparkled with mirth. Yup, he was trouble with a capital "T" and had been from the first moment she'd met him. He was the first man who had even gotten close to breaking down the brick wall she'd erected around her heart after Ryan was killed in action.

"Fine. But it has to be quick. There's no way I'm going to be picnicking while potential buyers are walking through the house. I do have a reputation, you know."

"Yes, ma'am, I'm very aware of your reputation," he answered with a salute and a grin. "Where do you want to eat?"

"The kitchen table, I guess. Please try not to make a mess. I have everything staged already, and I want it to stay that way."

He nodded, then flashed her a bright white smile and disappeared around the corner into the kitchen. The house was ready; she was ready—well except for the unplanned lunch break. A quick check of her watch told her she could probably eat at least half of the deliciousness waiting for her in the kitchen as long as she kept her hands off of Ethan and focused on the sandwich. The open house was supposed to start at one, so they had fifteen minutes to eat before "show time."

***

Ethan unpacked the food as he glanced around the kitchen. He tried to pick out what she'd added to help with the sale versus what was already there. He'd gotten good at finding her "special touches." She had a knack for making every home look welcoming, which was probably why she was the most sought-after realtor in Willow Haven.

He was glad he'd trusted his gut and brought lunch. He knew she wouldn't have eaten. It was her standard argument—she was too busy. As a bonus, he'd be able to check things out without her getting suspicious. As he unpacked the bag, his mouth watered. Iced coffee for her and sweet tea for him, two roast beef sandwiches, potato salad, and brownies for dessert.

"Are you coming?" he yelled for her as he finished unwrapping the food. If she waited much longer, she'd say she didn't have time and wouldn't eat at all. Not that he'd mind eating the rest her meal. But it defeated the whole purpose. Since he had the day off, he'd gone for his usual ten-mile run on the beach before the summer crowds gathered for the day. He loved the peacefulness of a sunrise run, just him, pelicans diving for fish, sandpipers digging for food, and the gentle lap of the waves against the shoreline.

"Why are you yelling?"

He looked up to see her standing in the doorway watching him. How long had she been standing there? From the way the skin was wrinkled between her eyes, she'd been thinking hard about something. About him, if he was lucky, but he wasn't counting on it. She was the most stubborn woman he'd ever met, and he'd met a few over the years.

"C'mon. Stop stalling."

"I'm not. I was just admiring the view."

He laughed and shook his head, and he pulled out a chair for her.

"Thank you, Ethan," she said as she lifted half of the sandwich and sniffed. Her look of pure bliss almost made him jealous, almost. It still didn't come close to the look on her face when she came apart in his arms. Just thinking about it made him squirm in his chair as the zipper of his jeans pushed against him. He could not get enough of her, and he doubted he ever would even if he spent every day with her.

They ate in silence. He was happy she hadn't tossed his ass out and just kept the food. It had been debatable as to whether she'd let him stay, and he was glad she had. It hadn't been easy to win her over. She was a hard nut to crack, and he'd done everything he could think of to try to get past the brick wall she'd built around her heart.

From the first time he'd seen her, Ethan knew he had to get to know her. At first, he was convinced it was lust, but it didn't take long for him to realize how special she was. And even less time to fall head over heels. And even though she wouldn't admit it, she felt the same way. He'd caught the look on her face when she didn't think he was watching too many times. But damn the woman wouldn't give an inch. So determined to not commit. Wasn't it supposed to be the guy who was afraid of commitment? What she didn't realize yet was that he was just as stubborn. When he decided on something nothing and no one would deter him, and he wanted her by his side for the rest of their lives.

They'd met while he was volunteering at the rehab clinic at the military hospital. After serving five years as a pilot in the Air Force, he couldn't just walk away from his brothers and sisters and volunteered as much as his schedule would allow. But he'd needed to get out. Too many close calls and lost friends convinced him it was time to get out before he lost himself. There were things he'd seen he'd never be able to share with anyone, and they'd left permanent scars on his soul. He still suffered from the nightmares almost every night. The evenings he spent with Anna helped. He figured the happiness helped to override the memories on those nights.

The clinic was usually busy, and the afternoon he'd first met Anna was no exception. It was one of those moments that you know will always be as crystal clear as when they happened. It was corny, and he'd never admit it to Steele, his partner on the job and best friend, but it was like she'd been surrounded by light and sparkles. He tried to blame it on the sun shining through the glass doors as she wheeled her brother into the building. It didn't take long for the bubble to pop when Tag mouthed off. He'd been a real son of a bitch then, but he hadn't been out of the hospital for long and was still learning how to deal with the loss of his leg and arm.

Ethan had been about to go over and tell the guy to lay off. But before he could walk away from the Vet he'd been working with, Anna told Tag he needed to get over himself, and she'd had enough of his bullshit. Unfortunately, it wasn't enough to stop the bitching coming out of Tag's mouth. He had to choke back a laugh when she'd turned around and left him in the middle of the check-in area and told him he could figure out another way home because she was too busy for his crap. She'd known exactly how to handle her brother—no pity. It was the best, they called it tough love, but really it was just telling him like it is, giving him the love he needed without babying him. Adjusting to losing a limb let alone two was never easy, but pity parties only made it worse, and Anna seemed to know that.

After that, he'd checked to see when Tag's sessions were and made sure he was there as often as possible, and then made a point of talking to her each time. The more he learned, the more he wanted to learn. It had taken two months, and three days before she agreed to a date. But who was counting? He had Tag to thank for it, too. Now it was a year later, and they were still moving at a snail's pace. He still couldn't get her to move in with him, leave some clothes at his place or let him leave some at her house. God forbid he should ask her to marry him. She'd probably get him booted out of town.

Tag told him she'd changed after the death of her fiancé. He'd been killed in action in Iraq. He'd volunteered for some secret mission and had never come home. It had pretty much destroyed her. He'd found out about Ryan's death about a month before the IED almost killed him. And once he and Mac got back stateside, she'd made it her personal missions to take care of both of them. But it was obvious to him that she wasn't the same Anna he'd grown up with. But he'd told Ethan not to give up on her either.

"Hey. Are you awake? What did you get?" Her question brought him back to the present, and he realized he'd been staring at her instead of eating.

"Sorry. I was thinking. I got the same thing as you."

"Couldn't resist the call of the roast beef, could you? Thank you for doing this. It's really great." She took another bite of the sandwich, and he suppressed a groan as her tongue slid across her lower lip to pick up a bread crumb. Damn, didn't she realize how sexy she was?

"Is everything okay?" Her question reminded him they didn't have all day for him to be mooning over her. And it proved she wasn't the hard-boiled business woman she tried to be, she still had a soft gooey center.

"Yup, everything's fine, and it's my pleasure, baby. Any opportunity for some extra time with you is perfect. I figured it was worth the shot."

"You're right. I'm sorry. There's always so much to do." Score. Win one for the Ethan man. She'd finally admitted she was working too much, at least he hoped that's what she'd meant. Maybe he was making headway.

Watching her eat was getting to be painful. He had it bad, and he knew it. They'd been together the other night, but his body couldn't get enough of her. He wanted to pull her out of her chair and into his arms. To kiss her soft lips, feel her fingers dig into his shoulders instead of the sandwich. Ugh. He needed a cold shower. Grabbing his sweet tea, he took a long drink to try to cool his rising libido. Now was definitely not the time. But later. Oh yeah, tonight would be different.

"Aren't you hungry?" Her big chocolate brown eyes focused on his face like she was searching for something.

"Hell yeah. Starving." He took a big bite, and she laughed. His eyes watered from the horseradish sauce he'd forgotten about. Damn. *Way to impress the lady, asshat.*

"Are you okay?" She couldn't hide the laughter in her voice.

"Funny, huh? Yeah, I'm fine, just forgot about the horseradish sauce. I even asked for extra. What was I thinking?"

"Obviously not about that." Her giggles made him happy. She spent too much time being serious.

"Obviously. How's yours?"

"Delicious as always. Dixie is amazing."

"Yes, she is. I hope she never decides to retire."

"You and me both. Willow Haven just wouldn't be the same. Dixie's Place has been here as long as anyone can remember."

"So, she was one of the original residents?"

"Her family was. They opened the little sandwich shop on the beach, but over the years it grew, and her parents bought the building she's in today."

"Was it always called Dixie's?"

"Yes. It was her great-great-grandmother's name, and there has been a woman from every generation who is named after her. Our Dixie is the fifth or sixth I think."

"Wow. That's cool. Does everyone know the history of this town like you do?"

"Probably not. I had it drummed into my head by my parents. It makes a better realtor if you know everything there is to know about the town. I doubt most people really care about half the stuff I know."

"Maybe, maybe not. You never know. I guess I'll have to start asking more questions."

"Okay, but not now. You need to eat. Time is ticking away." It was so easy to lose track of time with her. He could listen to her voice for hours, it was like smooth satin against his ears. He needed to concentrate, and by that, he meant eat his lunch and not stare at the women in front of him.

"How long is the open house?"

"Until four. Then I'll have to go back to the office for a bit."

"I thought I would cook for us tonight. If you give me the keys and alarm code, I'll bring everything over to your place and have it ready when you get home?"

"Umm, how about yours and I'll be over as soon as I can?"

"No way, I'm vetoing that option. I know you'll be in the office until at least seven. It's how you are, and I'd end up getting a phone call saying you worked too late and went to bed."

Her eyes widened, then she arched an eyebrow. "You think you have me down, huh?"

"Yup. I know you want to see me. What I can't understand is why you always have to fight it so hard." As soon as the words were out of his mouth, he wanted to take them back or kick himself, or maybe both. It was definitely not the time for this discussion, even if they needed to talk about it. They'd been dating for a year. He wanted more, and she kept holding back.

Her gaze turned frosty, and hints of gold glittered in the chocolate brown depths of her eyes. A sure sign she was pissed off. Why couldn't he learn to keep his mouth shut? "I'm sorry. I know it's not the time..."

"You're right, it's not. We need to clean up. I'm sure I'll have buyers here soon." And that was that. With one comment, she closed up tighter than an oyster, and he had no one to blame but himself.

"Anna, look..."

"It's okay, I get it. I do. But I have to work now."

"Okay. But I am sorry. I'll have dinner ready by seven." She was already standing and wrapping up the rest of her sandwich. At first, she didn't answer, and he figured he was fucked, and she'd back out of their date. But after a long—too long—sip of her iced coffee, her eyes met his, and they'd softened again. Thank God. Maybe he hadn't fucked it up totally yet.

"What are you making? Do you want me to stop and get anything on my way?"

"It's a surprise. And nope, I'll have everything we need."

"Should I be worried?"

"Babe, where's your sense of adventure?" But he already knew and wasn't surprised when she raised that expressive eyebrow again as she took another sip.

The sound of a car parking in front of the house ended their little interlude. But Ethan figured the way it had been going it was for the best. He needed to do some major damage control later, or he might as well flush all the progress he'd been making right down the toilet. If nothing else, Anna kept him on his toes.

Lynne St. James

CHAPTER TWO

It was after five by the time the last couple left, but she was pleased with the turnout. It had been a successful open house, and Anna was sure one or two couples would put in an offer before the week was out. Even though she was exhausted from being "on" all afternoon, it was a good tired, not like when she'd spent the afternoon poring over documents. In lots of ways, she missed the selling and interactions, but the business was so big it needed all of her time to keep things running smoothly.

She'd really hoped that Tag would decide to come on board, especially after he was discharged, but he'd found his purpose finally, and she was excited when they'd found the perfect property for his new rehabilitation facility or as he kept calling it his Double R—rehab ranch. It hadn't been open for long, but he and Mac really put a lot of time and energy into making it the perfect place for not only physical therapy but helping Vets with PTSD. Of course, that meant she was on her own with Willow Haven Realty, at least for now.

With a sigh, she double-checked that everything was back to the way she'd found it and set the lockbox on the door. As she grabbed the sign from the front lawn and headed toward her car, she noticed a guy leaning against the side of an old rusted-out green pickup truck. Their eyes met, and the hair on the back of her neck stood at attention. There was something sinister about the way he was staring at her.

When she looked up again after putting the signs in the trunk of her car, he was still there and still watching her. Not anxious to see if he was going to be trouble, she got into the car and made sure to lock the doors. She glanced up hoping he'd be gone, and that the entire thing had been her imagination, but it wasn't. Instead, he was still staring at her. Even from across the street, she picked up on his menacing vibes, there was real hatred there. But they didn't know each other so it couldn't be directed toward her, could it? While she watched, he flicked his cigarette. Her gaze followed the glowing ember as it arced in the air before bouncing on the asphalt. With one last look in her direction, he climbed into his truck and pulled away.

For a few seconds, she contemplated calling Ethan but talked herself out of it. "You're overreacting." The neighborhood was quiet, no one else was out, and he was just grabbing a smoke.

Since she was the only other person around, of course, he'd be watching her. Maybe she needed to stop watching all the Criminal Minds reruns.

Even though she didn't call Ethan, she couldn't shake the feeling that something wasn't right. She'd never seen the guy before that she could recall. Why would he be watching her? Trying to shake off the 'willies,' she decided not to take any chances he might follow her and turned down every side road possible on her way to the office, even going so far as to drive by the police station. After not seeing any sign of the truck, she pulled into the office parking lot.

The office was deserted, but considering it was after six on a Saturday, she wasn't surprised. Most open houses were done by four, and the agents went home from there. But this one had run late, very late and then with clean up, she was running behind—again. Just like Ethan said would happen.

Jenny only worked until four. For the most part being a realtor was a lot like being self-employed, at least the way she ran the business. No micromanaging for her. She despised it, so she sure as hell wasn't going to do it to anyone else. It was one of the first changes she'd made when she'd taken over, and morale had soared.

She stopped by Jenny's desk to check for messages then went into her office. Seeing the mountain of paperwork on her desk was like being doused with a bucket of ice water. It was the last thing she wanted to deal with after the busy afternoon. Knowing Ethan was already at her house preparing dinner sealed the deal. "Screw it. It waited this long, it can wait until Monday." Nodding at her decision, she leaned the signs against the wall, put her go-bag on one of the chairs, locked the office, and left.

The sun was still shining, and she stopped to grab her sunglasses from her purse after locking the front door of the building. That's when she noticed the truck, at least she thought it was the same truck. Was it a figment of her overactive imagination? Her mother always told her she should be an author since her imagination was out of control. Funny, she hadn't remembered that until just then. But it really did look like the same run-down truck. It was too far away for her to get the license plate, and she hadn't thought to check for it while at the open house. Were there that many old green pickup trucks in Willow Haven? Maybe. But it was weird that out of the blue today she was noticing them. If it was the same truck, where was the guy?

As she'd learned in her self-defense class, she checked her surroundings. Taking the class had been a knee-jerk reaction to losing control of everything in her life after Ryan was killed. But it was good to know, especially since she spent so much time alone, or had until she met Ethan.

After a quick scan of the parking lot, she hurried toward her car, she slid in and locked the doors. Once again, she was tempted to call Ethan but felt silly. He'd be busy making dinner and waiting for her to show up. What could he do anyway? She did decide to drive past the truck and try to read the license plate number. Better safe than sorry.

No sooner had she started her car when the truck peeled away from the curb. Coincidence? She didn't think so, and it reinforced her uneasiness. Why was he following her? For that matter, who the hell was he? She couldn't remember ever seeing either him or the truck before. Had she just been oblivious to her surroundings? Goosebumps rose on her arms. Was he watching her before today? Did he know where she lived?

For once she was glad she'd listened to her parents and had the alarm system installed at her house. Along with the self-defense classes, she should be okay, right? Taking a circuitous route home, she wondered whether to tell Ethan. She was most likely making a big deal out of nothing and needed to lay off the Tami Hoag books for a while. But it didn't stop her from routinely checking her rearview mirror for any sign of the green truck or its creepy driver.

Worried that he'd follow her home, she took the most out of the way route hitting every back road possible. It turned a ten-minute ride into twenty and pretty much ensured no one had followed her. It was a good thing she knew Willow Haven like the back of her hand, or she'd probably have gotten lost. By the time she got home, she was convinced she'd probably blown the whole thing out of proportion. Just because she'd seen the truck twice in one day didn't mean he was following her, it wasn't like the town of Willow Haven was huge. Maybe he lived in the neighborhood or was a guest, and they wouldn't let him smoke inside. When she thought about it that way, it made much more sense than a stranger following her, especially after there was no sign of him since she'd left the office.

As she turned into her driveway, she pulled past Ethan's car and into her garage. It had been thoughtful of him to pull over to the side so she could pull inside. Turning off the car as the door closed behind her, she took a deep breath. It had been a long day, longer still after she'd gotten herself all worked up, and taken the scenic route home.

The garage door was unlocked since Ethan was waiting for her. She pushed it open and stepped inside the mudroom. A mouthwatering aroma stopped her in her tracks. She inhaled again as she tried to figure out what he'd made. Until today, she hadn't even realized he could do much more than steaks or burgers on the grill. But the fantastic array of scents proved otherwise.

"Oh my God, Ethan, it smells amazing…" she said stepping through the kitchen doorway and stopping short as she saw him holding his phone to his ear.

As soon as he saw her, his face lit with a huge smile and held up a finger. Nodding, she pointed toward the bedroom. She might as well change out of her work clothes and let him finish his call. She hoped he wasn't being called in for work. It hadn't happened often, but it had happened. As much as she fought against their relationship, if she was honest with herself, she had to admit that she couldn't imagine him not in her life, even if she wasn't ready to tell him or move on to the next level. She was sure once he found out she cared for him, he wouldn't let up until she agreed to either move in with him or let him move in with her. And she wasn't ready for that. It was too close to how things had gone with Ryan. He'd moved in when he was home on leave, and then never returned. Nope, she definitely wasn't ready for another man to move in, but maybe she'd let him stay the night this time. That was progress, right?

***

"God dammit. Another one? Do you need me to come in?" Ethan asked his lieutenant as he heard the garage door open. Anna was finally home. He'd been waiting for her to call him all afternoon expecting her to cancel, after their little "thing" over lunch. When he hadn't heard from her, he was glad. But now after getting this call, he couldn't be happier to know she was finally home and safe.

For most of the time, he'd been on the job in Willow Haven it had been nice and quiet, exactly what he'd wanted and needed after his five years in the Air Force. But over the last two months, there had been a rash of burglaries. All the homes had been empty, and most were for sale with the owners either away or already moved out, except one where the couple had returned early from vacation in time to see a panel van pull out of the driveway. Unfortunately, they hadn't been able to identify anyone or even know if there was more than one person. Whoever was behind this had been careful not to leave any evidence behind.

He and his partner, Steele Brennan, had caught the first case, and at the time thought it was a simple B&E, or maybe the neighborhood kids getting some kicks. But they'd discovered soon enough that the robberies were well-planned—not a group of bored teenagers looking for trouble. After that first one, there had been another one every weekend just like clockwork. Two months and eight, err now nine, burglaries later, and they were no closer to solving them. They had to catch a break soon. Ethan was a firm believer that everyone fucked up eventually, and they'd be there to catch them. He just hoped no one got hurt before they did.

They'd been lucky the press hadn't made a big deal of the break-ins, and he would bet fifty bucks it was because there was nothing exciting about the robberies. It did make it easier for him to keep from discussing it with Anna.

She had plenty to handle without worrying about her staff getting robbed or worse. It was part of the reason he'd made sure to stop by the open house earlier. Not that he wanted her to think he was checking on her. Oh, fuck no. An avalanche of crap would have rained down on his head if he even implied she couldn't take care of herself. Since He and Steele hadn't figured out the timeframe for the break-ins, they were worried one of them would happen when someone was home. The only thing they had so far that even slightly resembled a lead was that all the houses were up for sale.

It's what bugged the shit out of him. How did they always know which house to hit and when? Steele thought someone was casing different neighborhoods in Willow Haven looking for vacant properties. Ethan had a feeling there was more to it, but he'd be damned if he'd been able to figure it out yet.

The crime scene called to him, it was like a puzzle he hadn't been able to figure out, and for him, that was damn frustrating. He should be there, but the LT said CSU and two other detectives, Davis and Harris had it covered. There weren't any witnesses other than the neighbor who'd seen lights on in the empty house and called it in. It was his case, and he should be there, but it was one of the biggest things in Willow Haven, so Ethan figured the LT wanted to give everyone a shot. But his gut twisted into a huge knot when he found out the address of the latest robbery—3232 Seashell Lane—the location of Anna's open house.

"What's wrong?" The case had him so deep in thought, he hadn't heard Anna come in.

"Nothing, babe. The LT called about one of my cases."

"Do you need to go? Can we eat first? I have to tell you though, whatever you made smells amazing. As soon as I opened the door, my mouth started watering. If I wasn't hungry before I'm starving now." She sounded surprised that he'd actually made something edible that didn't involve the grill, but he'd never told her it's what he did to relax. Cooking was therapy and the first thing he did when he was stressed. But usually, he'd donate the meals to the town homeless shelter instead of eating them; the preparation was what he enjoyed. Eating gourmet meals alone? Not so much. This was the first time he'd cooked for a date unless he counted the barbequing he'd done. He didn't, grilling was easy, coming up with complex sauces and layering of flavors was the challenge. Hopefully, he'd impress this woman who'd had chefs prepare her meals for a lot of her life.

"Nope. I don't need to go. Dinner is chicken in a white wine reduction with shallots and served on a bed of mushroom and garlic risotto. I have a fresh spinach salad with crumbled bacon, red onions, grape tomatoes, and blue cheese with a raspberry vinaigrette. I also picked up some rolls at Dixie's when I grabbed lunch. I knew I wouldn't have time to bake."

"You made all of this by yourself? Wait, you bake bread?" The stunned look on her face made him laugh and helped to shove the case into the dark recesses of his mind. He'd take it out and examine it later when she was sleeping. Overnight was when he did most of his thinking when the world was quiet, and his memories couldn't hurt anyone.

"Yup, I learned from my grandmother when I was really young. Over the years, I've taken a few cooking classes. But you know, you don't have to act so surprised. I'm not a Neanderthal." When her cheeks tinged with pink, he felt bad. He hadn't meant to embarrass her only tease her a little.

"I know you're not. I've never met anyone who could make bread from scratch, well, except for Dixie. But no one 'regular.' My mother can barely boil water. Tag and I would probably have starved if there hadn't been a cook when we were growing up. It wasn't on my mother's list of important life skills."

"Gran and Mom did all the cooking. I don't remember a time when she didn't live with us. After she passed away while I was in high school, it was never the same at home. I think she helped keep the family together."

"I'm so sorry." Anna put her hand on his lower arm and squeezed, sympathy evident in her eyes. He hadn't thought about his family in a long time. They were all gone now. The only one who he'd really cared about was his grandmother anyway.

"It's okay. I haven't thought about her in a while. Anyway, I'm glad you're hungry. Want to grab the wine and meet me at the table?" he said as he pointed to the wine bottle he'd opened earlier to let it breathe.

"Sure, anything to get the food to the table faster. Can I help with anything else?"

"As a matter of fact, there is something you can do." Before she had a chance to ask what, he'd wrapped his hands around her waist and pulled her against his chest. Then he tilted her chin so he could gaze into her hazel-brown eyes; they were more green than brown at that moment. "You can kiss me. I'm suffering from Anna withdrawal."

"Oh yeah?" She batted her eyes and grinned. "I think I might be able to help with that."

The first touch of her lips set him aflame. It was always the same—spontaneous combustion—and it never ceased to surprise him. That she wouldn't admit the spark between did, though, and it bugged the crap out of him. No other woman had even come close. From the first time, they'd kissed he'd known she was special. When they'd finally made love, it sealed the deal for him. She was it, there would never be another woman for him. His fate had been written.

Her arms slid around his neck as he deepened the kiss and she melted into his embrace. Forgotten was dinner, the break-ins, everything but the amazing woman in his arms. Soft, hot, but firm in all the right places. There would never be a time when he'd have his fill of kissing her. He was about to lift her up and carry her to the bedroom and say, 'fuck dinner' when she pulled back. His disappointment had to show on his face.

"I really am starving, and the food smells too good to waste. Let's eat and then we can have dessert." Her smile and wink softened the rejection he'd felt when she broke their kiss. She was right, they were adults, weren't they? But a little spontaneity never hurt anyone, but would he ever be able to convince her of that?

With another quick kiss to her forehead, he pusher her toward the dining room, while he went to get the food from the kitchen. He already had the table set, so it was just a matter of serving her. He'd even remember to get a bouquet of lilacs and orange blossoms—her favorite flowers. The final touch were the candles he'd found in her cabinets. The look of wonder on her face assured him that he'd nailed it. Romance might not be his middle name, but it didn't mean he couldn't pull it off when he wanted. The appreciation on her face was all the encouragement he needed.

"Oh, Ethan, you really went for it. The table is beautiful. I can't believe you even bought flowers. I don't know what to say."

"Baby, this is just me showing you that you mean the world to me. You're the first woman I've cooked for besides my mother and grandmother. Hopefully, that tells you something."

"Thank you." She came over and stood on tip toes and kissed him. It was soft, gentle, and over almost before it started. But for the first time, there was a promise in the kiss. Maybe her hard shell was finally cracking—at least a little.

Lynne St. James

CHAPTER THREE

"What do you want to do now?" Anna asked as they put the last of the leftover food in the refrigerator and finished clearing the dishes. Their usual Saturday night dates were dinner out and either a movie or a walk on the beach followed by coffee. Ethan had gone above and beyond. It was by far the most romantic thing anyone had ever done for her. Her heart melted into a big puddle of goo when she'd seen the table set with flowers and candles, and not just any flowers but her favorites.

Ethan told her weekly to stop fighting her feelings, and stop holding back. She had been, he was right even if she didn't want to admit it. But she couldn't help it. Too many hard lessons in such a short period of time made her gun shy. It was easier to be alone and lonely than fall in love and go through another devastating loss. Did it mean she was a coward? Maybe, but Ryan's death was devastating. She'd believed they were soulmates, had been together since high school.

Thinking about him brought tears to her eyes, or had. For the first time, she realized she'd been thinking about Ryan and wasn't teary-eyed. The familiar heart twisting pain in her chest wasn't there either. All that was left was melancholy for what could have been. Had she finally healed the broken pieces of her heart? Healed? Maybe taped back together, but if it was, it was because of Ethan. He'd been responsible for drawing her out. Not taking no for an answer. Making her have fun again. But did that mean she was ready to fall in love again?

Ethan had a dangerous job as a detective. No, they weren't in a big city, but still. He put his life in danger every day he was on the job, just like Ryan, just like Mac and Tag, and she'd almost lost them too. She should be dating a gardener, then she'd only have to worry about a runaway lawn mower. Just the thought made her giggle.

"What's so funny?"

"Nothing, really. Just a funny thought."

"Want to share?"

"Not this time, sorry."

"Well okay then. Be that way. So, as I was asking, how about a movie?"

"What?"

"Babe, you okay? Didn't you just ask me what I wanted to do now?" Crap, she had.

"Yeah, I did, sorry. I guess I was daydreaming, or maybe it was too much wine and excellent food.

You really outdid yourself. I had no idea you could cook like that."

"I'm glad you liked it." He stepped behind her, and his large hands massaged the tight muscles of her shoulders.

"Oooh, that feels good."

"You seem a little tense. How about instead of the movie, I give you a massage?"

"Is that code for let's go to bed?" It had been a long day, and making love with Ethan all night long definitely sounded better than a movie. Then she remembered creepy dude. Shit, just thinking about him made her tense even more.

His fingers stilled for the space of a few heartbeats before continuing to coax the knots from her neck. "Not really, but I wouldn't turn it down if you're offering. You just tightened up like a violin string. What's going on?"

"Nothing really."

"Anna..."

Ugh, she hated when he used that tone. It reminded her of Tag when they were younger. He would catch her at something and use that same tone, followed quickly by the threat to tell their parents if she didn't 'fess up.'

"It was just a long day."

He didn't believe her, he didn't have to say it for her to know. They'd been dating for almost a year and whether she wanted to admit it or not they knew each other a lot better than she'd ever known Ryan. It was crazy really since she'd grown up with him, but he'd always had another side to him, one he didn't share with her or anyone as for as she knew.

But Ethan was an open book. He'd even told her about his time in country and how it affected him. She hadn't known Ryan was in Army Intelligence until Tag told her afterward, and how he knew she had no idea. Secrets, they sucked. Lies were worse. But so far, Ethan had been nothing but up front.

"Okay, so you won't tell me. Do you think it will make me mad?"

"No, I would rather not ruin our wonderful evening talking about it. We can discuss it tomorrow. Deal?"

He turned her so she'd be facing him, and he searched her face for something. Whatever he was looking for he'd obviously found it, because he gave her one his sexiest smiles. "Deal. Hmmm, now, where were we? Oh yeah, a massage."

Before she could say a word, the room tilted as he picked her up and headed for her bedroom. "I'm perfectly capable of walking."

"Mmmm hmmm."

"I'm too heavy to carry."

"Are you kidding me? You're light as a feather."

"Excuse me, I think you've had too much wine, dude. I'm five foot eight. I *am* not a feather."

"You are to me."

She was about to answer when his lips covered hers. His tongue teasing until she let him in. He tasted like wine and sex and smelled like pure man with a hint of his citrus aftershave. All she wanted was his hands on her—everywhere—right now. He deepened the kiss, and somehow a soft moan escaped. His chuckle against her lips sent a sizzle of electricity to her core.

The urge to be snarky was quickly tamped down when he nipped at her lips as he pulled back. "Why are you stopping?"

"Do you want to have sex in the hallway? I kinda thought you'd prefer the bed or at least the couch. But hell, woman, I'll take you against the wall if that's what you want."

Damn, one kiss and her brain turned to mush. "Bed, now. Chop, chop, detective. I need you."

"Yes, ma'am."

***

If he'd realized that cooking for his woman would trigger this tigress, he'd have offered to cook for her months ago. Playful, sexy, demanding. If the wall around her heart wasn't down, it was crumbling, and he was going to bulldoze right through it.

He contemplated tossing her onto the bed but changed his mind. Instead, he slid her down his body so she'd have no doubt how much he wanted her. His Goddamn pants were on the verge of busting open. If they got any tighter, he'd be a soprano for a few days.

"Mmm. Is that for me?"

"Do you really have to ask?"

"No, but I want to hear you say it. Tell me how much you want me." He liked this Anna. It just might be time to start up a personal catering business, and by personal it would be Anna only.

"Oh, I want you, woman, from the top of your head to the tip of your toes and everything in between. Touching you, kissing you, breathing in your scent. You drive me crazy. I can't think of anything but having you."

A spark of mischief gleamed in her eyes. It was all the warning he had. She reached for the collar of his shirt and then ripped it open. Buttons pinged as they bounced across the wood floor of her bedroom. The zipper of his jeans dug into his most sensitive skin, and he groaned. These pants had to go, or he was sure he'd have a permanent scar. They needed to be naked.

It was taking too long. He loved that she was taking the aggressor role, but he couldn't wait another second. He pushed her backward onto the bed and shrugged out of what was left of his shirt. After ripping open his jeans, he kicked them across the room. Her urgency was contagious, and he needed to be buried deep inside her.

Her eyes caressed his body as they traveled its length, and she licked her lips when she got to the proof of his arousal. As the pink tongue slid along the smooth skin of her lips, it left a trail of shiny wetness. With another groan, he'd reached the limit of his endurance. Enough teasing.

"Up, woman, you need to get out of that dress. Unless you want me to tear it off of you?"

"You wouldn't."

"Try me."

She hesitated for a moment, and he thought she was going to tell him to go ahead, but some of his old Anna was still in there. Scooting to the edge of the bed, she stood up and pulled the dress over her head. He'd expected a bra and panties, what he got was nothing. Five feet eight inches of sun-kissed skin and nothing else. Holy shit.

"Damn. You were naked all through dinner?"

"Not naked. I was wearing the dress."

"You might as well have been, and I wasted it."

"Nope, but you're wasting it now," she said and put her hands on her hips and posed. Yup, there was going to be a lot more cooking in his future.

Tossing the pillows and the comforter to the floor, he picked her up, slid her onto the bed, and followed her down. The time for words was over.

He'd really wanted to go slow, planned to make it a tender seduction, kissing and worshipping every inch of her body. With actions if not words, he would prove how much he loved her. He hadn't said the words yet, but it was the truth, and his heart knew it. Before tonight he'd have sworn she wasn't ready, but now he wasn't so sure. Still, he didn't want to push her away either. But he also didn't want to scare her away. So instead he loved her with his body, hands, and mouth. Cherished every inch until she begged him for release. Then he pushed her further, poured out his love for her with every kiss, every lick, every thrust until they saw stars. Then he started all over again.

***

The sun peeking through the curtains woke him. For the first time in more years than he wanted to think about, he'd slept through the night. No nightmares at all. No waking up in a cold sweat, shaking, the scent of fear choking him as he watched the plane hit the ground in an explosion of flames, spewing twisted metal and body parts. Moondog's body parts. Shaking his head, he didn't want to dwell on it now, not when he'd finally not relived it in a dream.

He needed to focus on the now, the fact that he was still in her bed. She hadn't kicked him out as usual. Instead, she was still tucked against him after hours of making love. A first for them. She'd been a 'definitely no sleepover' kind of girl. Whatever had changed he was thankful. A huge step forward in their relationship, or whatever she'd decided to call it this week.

Unable to resist her tousled appearance, he kissed her slightly-parted lips. So warm, so soft, so beautiful. He wanted her—again. Twice last night was not enough, he'd never have his fill of her. If it weren't for the dark smudges under her eyes, he'd covered her body in kisses until she woke.

Instead, he'd make coffee and see what she had in the way of breakfast fixings. He wouldn't wake her with his body, but he couldn't be held responsible if the scent of fresh coffee and bacon woke her up, now could he?

Carefully sliding out of her arms so as not to wake her, he had a hard time finding is jeans in the discarded clothing and bed linens. He salvaged the pants, but the shirt was hopelessly shredded and ready for the rag pile. As quietly as possible he searched her bathroom for some toothpaste, wishing like hell he'd thought to bring a toothbrush with him, and a change of clothes for that matter. But he'd never had to worry about any of this before. It wasn't the first and wouldn't be the last he'd had to use his finger to brush his teeth. It was quick and dirty but better than nothing.

Devoid of morning breath, he hoped, he went in search of her coffee pot and beans. He knew she was a coffee snob, so he wasn't surprised to find a French press and grinder tucked into the "appliance garage" in the corner of her countertop. He loved her kitchen. It was a chef's dream, high-end everything, and she hardly ever used it from what he could tell. But it was easy to have the best, she came from a very wealthy family, and had earned plenty of her own money since she'd assumed control of the realty. From what he'd heard around town, it had more than tripled in size since she'd taken over, she'd even opened satellite offices in adjoining towns. Her father should be proud, but instead, he was just a jerk.

The bean grinder was sure to wake her, so he put that off until the water was ready. Then he searched for the leftover bacon he'd put in the fridge the night before, grabbed the eggs and some cheese. After going through what she had and what was left from the night before he whipped up a quiche and tossed it in the oven.

He'd always objected to the "real men don't eat quiche" comment. They were stupid if they didn't. Not for the first time, he wondered if he'd missed his calling. Maybe he should have opened a restaurant when he'd gotten out of the Air Force, but then he loved helping people too. Besides, if he kept getting reactions like last night, he'd be happy to reserve his cooking for his woman.

After the water was ready, he ground the beans and set up the French press. It would have to sit for a bit for the beans to be infused into the water before he'd be able to push the plunger and have coffee. Five minutes always felt like forever when you were waiting for the coffee, but he knew from experience it would be worth every second. He got out the half-and-half and sugar since he knew that's how she liked her coffee. He took his black, and if you listened to his partner, Steele, it was just like his soul. The stronger, the better, but after getting a good night's sleep, he wouldn't need coffee sludge today.

"Coffee. Is it ready yet?"

"Yes, ma'am. Good morning, beautiful." She looked good enough to eat, but he'd hold off until they had their coffee. It was the gentlemanly thing to do. After all, it had been their first night together. "I hope you don't mind, but I made breakfast."

"Mind? It smells delish. What did you make?"

"Quiche." As expected, she giggled, and it was heaven to his ears. Sweet, joyful and totally Anna.

"What? Real men do eat quiche, and you damn well know I'm right."

A hint of a blush graced her cheeks as she smiled. After their antics last night, he'd have been surprised if she hadn't blushed. She'd been a wild woman.

"Did you sleep okay? I know that sometimes in strange beds…"

"It was great. Your bed is wonderful and perfect because I got to share it with you."

"About that…"

Damn, when would he learn to keep his mouth shut? "What about it?" he said and poured coffee into the two mugs he had pulled out earlier. He slid hers across the counter toward her. Then he inhaled the scent before having his first taste.

"I think the no sleepover rule is kind of stupid, how about you?" He sipped his coffee, but inside he did a fist pump and shouted, 'wahoo.' It hadn't been wishful thinking; he was winning her over. Now he just had to be careful not to push too hard too fast.

"I've never been so happy to break a rule, and I vote for putting it down the garbage disposal."

"All right then. I guess I know where you stand."

"Baby, I never agreed with the rule to begin with. But I didn't want to push you into something you weren't ready for and run the risk of losing you.

If you haven't figured it out yet, I've fallen in love with you." Ugh. There he did it, it was bound to slip out sooner or later. Cringing inside, he waited for her response, half expecting her to tell him to get out and get over himself.

Her eyes widened, the brown getting more hazel like it did when she was full of emotion. But what was she feeling? "You're in love with me?"

"Yes. You really didn't know, did you?"

"I guess. I don't know. I think I was avoiding the entire subject. God knows you are persistent enough."

"Only when it's something I want. And I want you. But I am trying hard to take it slow. And I'm not sure what happened yesterday to change your way of thinking. But I'm ecstatic. And there is no way I'm letting you backslide, so don't even think about it."

"Don't worry. It's all good. And for the record, I loved sharing my bed with you."

"Does that mean I can move in?"

"Don't push it, buddy! Take your win and enjoy it…for now."

Before he could say anything else, the buzzer dinged, and it was time to eat. The alarm reminded him he hadn't checked his phone. He'd bet there was an update from the LT or Steele. Breakfast was ready, and he was still technically off-duty so it could wait. He didn't want to do anything to ruin this moment with Anna. He'd been waiting too long and worked too hard to gain her trust. If she found out about the investigation, he wasn't sure how she'd react. They'd have to discuss it eventually, especially since yesterday's break in was related to her and her business.

Chapter Four

Expecting to wake up and feel the mistake of last night cringing in her stomach, Anna was surprised and the overwhelming feeling of happy when she opened her eyes. The first thing she thought of wasn't, "Oh my God, what did I do?" Instead, she stretched and enjoyed the slight soreness of her well-loved body. He'd kept his word and loved every inch of her, and when they'd finished and caught their breath, he started again.

He had to have put something in the food. She'd never heard of an aphrodisiac in chicken or salad, but damn there had to be something. All of her reservations about their relationship just up and left, seemed to fade into the ether. Probably where they had belonged anyway. But even she wasn't sure what caused her change of heart, no wait, it wasn't her heart it was her head. Or was it? Damn, as hard as she'd tried, she had fallen for him. The slippery little sucker slid right into her heart without her noticing. And now she couldn't wipe the shit-eating grin off her face.

It was Sunday, the one day she didn't go into the office, but her staff did. There were lots of open houses and buyers who could only shop on the weekends. When she took over the business, she'd tried opening one Sunday a month to see how it went. Now they were open every Sunday. Which reminded her that she needed to call in and check how things were going.

After helping Ethan clean up after breakfast, they settled on the couch in the living room. She flipped on the TV, and they grabbed their phones to check on work. She'd never realized just how sexy a man could be in only a pair of jeans, sprawled out on the couch. Dang. He was wreaking havoc on her concentration and her body. It took all her willpower not to lean over and run her tongue across his washboard abs. She must have been in some kind of a daze not to have noticed them before. Although, they hadn't spent any time together outside of the bedroom without being fully dressed. She'd stick to that excuse for being temporarily blind to his many assets. *Oh God. He's not wearing a shirt because I ripped it apart last night.* Her face was so hot it had to be glowing three shades of red. Thank goodness, he was distracted by whatever he was reading on his phone. Hopefully, he wouldn't notice. Shaking her head at her ridiculousness, she caught sight of the TV.

"Hey. That's my office." She grabbed the remote and turned up the volume.

The female reporter was outside of the Willow Haven Realty building. "...The house that was broken into was 3232 Seashell Lane. I contacted the Willow Haven Police Department for a statement, but Lieutenant Mark Watson said at this time they had no statement but promised a press conference tomorrow afternoon. A person who didn't wish to be identified said this is one of a string of robberies that have occurred lately. That's all for now. Reporting live for KHTZ News this is Sam Watson."

Anna turned toward Ethan who was staring at the TV like it had grown a second head. "Do you know what she's talking about? I can't believe I was in that house yesterday. I wonder if it will affect the sale? Duh. Of course, it will."

Ethan had a weird look on his face as he turned from the television screen to face Anna. At first, he didn't say anything. A myriad of emotions crossed his face, the last looking a bit like guilt. What did he know?

"The call I was on when you got home last night? It was the LT telling me about the break-in. Steele and I have been working this case."

"And you didn't tell me about it? Don't you think it might have been good for me to know?"

"No, well yes. But it's work. I can't just talk about open cases we're investigating. And before you say another word, you were never a suspect. But we don't know who is, we're still running down leads."

"But this is one my houses. How long has this been going on?"

"Anna, baby, I really can't talk about this. Well beside the part you're involved in. We've been lucky to keep it out of the news, but it was bound to break eventually. I was really hoping we'd be able to solve this and you'd never have to know."

"How long?" When he didn't answer at first, irritation forced her to her feet. Frustration, followed by anger sent her into the kitchen. She needed time to think. It was his work, they didn't—couldn't discuss his open cases, for just that reason, they were open. She shouldn't be pissed off at him for not sharing this, but irrational or not she was still pissed. What if Adria had been there when they broke in?

"It's an ongoing case. We had a deal remember? We don't talk about work when we're on our date—unwind time, right?"

"I know but, dammit, Ethan. What if Adria was there yesterday? She could have been hurt, or worse."

"Do you think I haven't been worried about that? Last night when I found out, my first instinct was to go to the crime scene. It could have been you. Not that Adria isn't important, but I'm not in love with her." He was right, she knew it, he knew it, but it didn't do much to take the edge off her anger.

"What can you tell me about the case, anything? I know there are rules, but I think you can do a little bending here."

"You do, huh? That's because you're the boss. But I discussed it with the LT, and he thinks you might be able to help us out."

"What could I do?"

"All the houses burglarized have been vacant and for sale. Well, except for one. The couple was selling the house, through your office in fact. They returned from vacation a few days early, because of bad weather, in time to see a van pulling out of their driveway. If they'd gotten home any earlier, they'd have walked in on the robbery."

"One of mine? All of them? How many houses?"

"Last night makes number nine."

"Nine! What the hell, Ethan. Nine houses and you didn't think I needed to know?"

"We've had extra patrols…"

"They've worked really well, apparently," she said, her voice dripped with sarcasm. None of this was his fault, well except the part where he didn't tell her—maybe—but he was the one in front of her, and she was angry, and he got to be "it."

"They might have worked. We don't know for sure," he said, anger building in his voice. "Do you want to know about the case or are you just going to throw snarky comments at me?"

He was right, pissed off or not, this wasn't helping either of them. "Yes, I want to know. How about some more coffee while we talk about it?" Her white flag retreat was accepted, and they both breathed a sigh as they realized they'd averted a huge argument. Adulting was hard, but someone had to do it.

Coffee made, they took their mugs and went onto the patio where the sound of running water from the waterfall on her pool helped to create a more Zen-like environment. She had a feeling she wasn't going to like where this was going and the more help with calm the better.

***

This was exactly why he hadn't told her last night. Thank God he'd kept his mouth shut. Too bad she'd put on the TV, though. It's not like he hadn't already planned to discuss it with her today. The LT had given him the go ahead because of her knowledge of the real estate scene in Willow Haven and that some of her listings were involved. But then it would have been on his terms, not the freakin' news.

He loved her backyard. Typical Florida, lots of flowers, orange and avocado trees and a beautiful pool that looked like it was part of a tropical oasis. It screamed money, and he wondered if they got married whether their different financial status would matter. Not that he'd be proposing any time soon. If she couldn't admit she was in love with him, even though it was plain for everyone to see, then he'd have to wait. Saying the words had been a spontaneous outburst, not that he was sorry he'd said them, only that she hadn't said it back.

Waiting until she was settled in one of the chaise lounges, he sipped his coffee and wondered where to start. She took care of that for him.

"Are all the houses our listings?"

"All but the first one and the one last Saturday night, so seven of the nine. Which is why the first one might have been a practice run." She nodded and waited for him to continue.

"We didn't think about the connection until two or three in, partly because with so many of the owners out of town and being older couples it wasn't always easy to get answers. Last week's robbery was a new listing, although not with your company, it was the only one that was for sale by owner."

"Seven? Holy shit. And never when anyone was there?"

"Exactly. When Steele and I were talking to the LT on Friday, we started to connect the dots. They're too well planned." As she nodded, he could almost see the wheels turning in her head. Knowing her analytical mind, she was probably running every possible scenario already.

"You think it's an inside job?"

She was quick, but then she had more information than they'd started with. Still, overall, he felt like he'd dropped the ball on this one. He should have put it together sooner. So much for 'protect and serve.' "Yes, maybe, possibly."

"Do you think it's me? Is that why you didn't say anything?"

"No! Of course not. I already said you weren't a suspect. How could I think it's you? Jesus Christ, Anna. C'mon, give me a little credit, will you? Besides, what would be the motive to steal from your listings? Face it, you have more money than you know what to do with." He could hardly contain the instant spark of anger that sent his blood pressure skyrocketing. So much for headway in their relationship.

"Sorry. But when you didn't say anything, and most of the houses were my listings…"

"You are not now or ever a suspect. Okay? But we can't rule out one of your employees. They all have access to the lockbox codes, right? And would know the schedules? Or at least be able to find them?"

"Yes, that's true. But most of them have been with the company for years, and we've never had this issue before."

"Have you hired anyone recently? Or has anyone had any financial difficulty?"

"No. My newest employee is Adria, and I know it's not her. You have to know it's not too. As far as financial troubles, I wouldn't know. How would I, unless they came to me to ask for a loan or help? I don't run financials on my employees." She worried her lower lip between her teeth, a sure sign she was focused on a problem. "Are you sure it's not just a bunch of kids looking for kicks?"

"At first, we thought that was a definite possibility. But no. There has been too much planning, precision, patience, in and out before anyone realizes. No damage to the home. Teenagers wouldn't be able to resist damaging something for the hell of it. The only way we find out is when either a neighbor calls the next day because the lockbox is off or lights are on."

"That's just bizarre."

"It feels like they are taunting us. But they're smart and careful. Not even a fingerprint has been left at the scene. They think they can't be caught, and that's when we'll get them. They'll get cocky and make a mistake, and we'll be waiting."

"But how many more homes have to be robbed first?"

"That's the issue. The LT thinks you can help us try to narrow it down."

"What can I do?"

"I'm going to give you all the addresses of the burglaries. Can you give us the files for your listings?"

"Yeah, but what are you looking for? Most of the stuff in our files are notes about the home, photographs for the listing, and the contract. We don't have a lot of specific information."

"We're looking for similarities between the properties."

"Okay, well I can do that now. Let me get my laptop. Since I computerized everything, it's all on our server."

"Who has access to that?"

"In the office? Everyone has access to some of the things, there are separate logins for each of the agents. The MLS is built into the system, and everyone has access to that."

"What's the MLS?"

"Multiple Listing Service. It's basically a huge database of all available homes, usually with pictures. It also gives information about upcoming open houses, caravans, and listing agents."

"Caravans?"

She rolled her eyes. "No, not what you're thinking. A caravan is a once-a-month occurrence when a bunch of real estate agents travel from one new listing to another to get a feel for all of the homes, etc. before they start showing them to their clients."

"Gotcha. All of your agents have access to that?"

"Yes, but not just mine. Any licensed real estate agent can get access to the realtor side, and then there is the public side."

"The public has the same access?"

"No. But the can see a listing of all of the homes for sale and the realtors to contract for more information to see the house."

"Fuck. I was hoping it would be easier to narrow it down."

"It might be. Let me get the laptop."

"While you're doing that I'll make more coffee."

"Perfect."

After starting the coffee, he called Steele to see if he'd heard anything new.

"Fuck, seriously dude? I don't get enough of you while we're at work?" Steele said and laughed. "I guess I should be happy I didn't hear from you last night. I figured after the LT called you'd be sending me a text to meet you at the scene."

"I thought about it, but I was at Anna's, and I was cooking."

"No way. It's about fucking time. I thought I was going to have to lock you two in a room until you could work out your shit."

"There was nothing to work out. I told you we were going slow."

"Bro, there's slow, and then there's fucked up. Do you need me to tell you which it was?"

Ethan laughed. He and Steele had hit it off in the academy and were lucky enough to get assigned as partners after they both made detective. He'd been his first friend outside of the Air Force and appreciated his blunt style, even if most people didn't.

"Just shut the fuck up already. I called for a reason, not an ass-reaming."

"Yeah, yeah. What's up?"

"I've been talking to Anna about the case, and we're going over her listings. Can you grab the files from the station and bring them over? We've got leftovers from last night's dinner, so I'll make it worth your while."

"Yeah, no problem. Did you check with your ball n' chain to see if it's okay?"

"Again, shut the fuck up. And you'd better be on your best behavior when you're here, or I'll toss you in the pool."

"I'm just busting you."

"I know that but Anna won't. She hasn't been around you like I have. You only met her the one time, and since it was at the station, you were sort of on your better behavior. I don't think you ever have a 'best' behavior."

"Fuck you. But yeah, you got it. I'll be a boy scout."

"Thanks. I appreciate it. Oh, can you bring a t-shirt too?"

"I'm not even going to ask, but yeah. See you in about an hour."

When he disconnected, he looked up to see Anna watching him from the end of the kitchen island. "Who was that?"

"Steele. He's bringing over our files and a shirt."

"Shit, I'm sorry." A blush stained her cheeks, and she avoided his gaze as she set up the computer and plugged it in.

"No sweat, baby. I didn't bring anything to change into that's all."

"Because you didn't know you were staying…"

"Exactly. But in the future, I'll be prepared."

"Ugh, you don't even have a toothbrush. I have spares, let me get one for you."

"Thanks, I appreciate it. I used my finger earlier, but it's not exactly the best implement for the job," he said and waggled his eyebrows making her laugh. Exactly his intention. Yeah, he had all the right implements for the important job, and if he had his way, he'd be using them again later.

CHAPTER FIVE

By the time Steele arrived, she'd explained to Ethan the difference between MLS and her listings and how it was all set up in her offices. Each of the agents had their logins to specific options, but only she and Jenny had access to everything—and Tag—but she doubted he'd be able to login even if he tried. She'd set him up with access since he was part owner of the business whether he wanted it or not, and she needed a backup person just in case. After what happened with Ryan she learned life was way too short.

Which of course made her feel even more stupid for pushing Ethan away for so long. Why did she think protecting her heart from hurt was better than living again? Sometimes she wondered at her own logic. Adria would tell her it was the pain talking. Since she still hadn't gone on even one date yet after being widowed over four years ago, she'd probably know all too well. Her usual excuse was Scotty, but it was just that—an excuse.

Anna showered and got dressed leaving Ethan to look through the listings for the seven houses that were hers. It wasn't long after she was done when the doorbell rang.

"I'll get it," he said, dropping a quick kiss on her lips before heading to greet his partner. She'd only met Steele once, but he seemed okay. Ethan warned her he could come off rude and crude, but not to take anything he said personally. She wasn't worried; she'd been dealing with Tag and all his shit for the last two years, so she was more than used to obnoxious males.

When they came into the kitchen, Anna was a little surprised. Seeing the two of them in the enclosed space took her breath away. They could have been cover models, but where Ethan was light, Steele was dark, foreboding, but hot damn he was hot. Her cheeks heated, and she was glad mind reading wasn't one of Ethan's many talents. It would have been just plain mortifying.

"Close your mouth, sweetheart. You might drool on the keyboard." Okay, maybe mind reading *was* one of his talents. Her cheeks had to be flaming now since her face was burning up.

Steele saved her, as he stepped forward to shake her hand. "Hi Anna, nice to see you again."

"Same here. Sorry to ruin your Sunday."

"Nah. I was bored anyway. Besides, I heard you had Ethan leftovers."

She laughed. "Hey, I thought you said you'd never cooked for anyone else."

"I said no other woman besides my mother and grandmother. You need to listen better, and you talk about me." He softened his words with a huge toothy grin.

"Whatever."

"Uh oh, bro, you're fucked now. She said that word," Steele said with a smirk.

"What word?"

"Whatever. Don't you go on Facebook? It's in one of these meme things, one of the four deadly words in a relationship. You need to pay more attention."

Anna couldn't stop laughing. She liked Steele better with every word he said and the more confused Ethan looked. It was hysterical, and she needed to remember to tell Adria about it when they were in the office tomorrow. Thinking of Adria made her wonder if Steele was single. She could picture the two of them together, and to have someone like Steele around, even with his cursing, would be good for Scotty, her son.

"I may be slow on Facebook, but I know that look when I see it. She's setting you up with one of her girlfriends. Look out, bud," Ethan said as he elbowed his partner in the side. Now they were both staring at her with scared expressions, and it was classic. Oh yeah, she had to figure out if he was single and then set him up with Adria. They'd be a great couple.

"I don't know what you two are talking about. But I thought we had work to do." Her comment had the anticipated effect, and they both sobered and got down to business. Steele pulled the files out his backpack and spread them over the top of the island. One by one they went over the information she had for each house that was one of her listings, marking off every possible combination of information from the date first listed, the home value and who initially listed the home.

After going through the seven listings that were hers, she brought up the MLS website and pulled the same information on the other two properties. Other than the MO they couldn't figure out the connection between the other two break-ins and her listings. What they finally discovered upset Anna, since they'd all been listed by Hugh Johnson and Adria Harrison.

Ethan and Steele were convinced it had to be Hugh since there was no way they could talk her into thinking Adria was involved. Hugh being involved didn't make sense to her either. He'd worked for them since her parents ran the company, and he had to be close to retirement age. A cranky old man? For sure. A criminal mastermind? No way. It surprised her that he'd been able to still get listings or even make sales, and she'd figured he must be more pleasant to the customers than his co-workers. Over the years, she'd had several complaints about his rudeness, mostly with the women in the office, but that was the extent of it. So again, none of this made sense.

It took them about three hours to go through everything while they debated back and forth about each and every piece of information. Anna wondered if this was how they always worked their cases and if so how they ever solved anything. But then again Willow Haven wasn't a hotbed of crime, at least until now. Ethan had told her that he'd decided to stay after his discharge because it was so quiet.

The guys went outside to the patio to come up with their plan of action while she heated dinner. Microwaving she usually could handle. But that was the extent of her prowess in the kitchen. No one could be good at everything, and growing up with a cook meant her mother never taught her the basics. Once she was older, she was too busy doing everything else and learning to cook was low on her priority list. But having a man who could cook was like a dream come true. There were only so many salads a girl could eat.

***

"You were right, she's a keeper. After listening to you bitch about how hard it was to get close to her, I wondered if it was really worth the effort, but yup. You got lucky. Now don't fuck it up and lose her." Steele imparted his sage advice as he paced the patio.

"Yeah, tell me something I don't know. I can't tell you the number of times I've almost fucked it up. But she's amazing, and I think my perseverance finally paid off."

"What are you persevering at?" Anna asked as she opened the French doors while juggling the platter of chicken.

"The case," Steele answered, and Ethan was grateful. He'd probably have put his foot in his mouth—again.

"Good because I really want you to find out who's behind it, and I know it's not Hugh. The sooner you get over that, the better."

"I think we should call Chase."

"Who's Chase?"

"My brother, he runs the Eagle Security and Protection Agency. Basically, a fancy name for a private security company."

"Why would we need private security?" Anna asked as she looked between the two of them. Steele might have a point. He could run things that they couldn't without a warrant.

"Because he doesn't have his hands tied while he waits for enough proof to get a warrant. Go ahead, give him a call, but I don't think we should tell the LT until we have something concrete because he's going to have our ass for this."

"No shit. But Chase is family, and an ex-SEAL if he's not trustworthy then who is?"

"He's an ex-SEAL?"

"Yeah. And before you decide to start matchmaking again, don't. He's had his panties in a twist for years for a woman he left behind in San Diego," Steele added.

"I don't think she's going to try matchmaking, you can relax, right, Anna?"

"Umm, sure, yup, right. I wouldn't dream of it." His woman had a very wicked gleam in her eyes, and if he didn't think it was so funny, he'd have to warn Steele to be on the lookout for women in his path.

While Steele went off to call Chase and see what he could dig up on her employees, Ethan had to propose their plan. She was going to hate it, of that he had no doubt. She protected her employees like a mother hen, which wasn't a bad thing, but in this case, it might mean she was assisting a felon.

"So, as far as Hugh is concerned, you have to at least admit that it's too much of a coincidence. I do agree about Adria. There's no way she's involved."

Steele was back before she had a chance to respond. "I told Chase to start with Hugh and Adria to be on the safe side. He'll call as soon as he has something. He has a computer guy who can find a flea in on a sheepdog."

Ethan didn't like the clouds building in Anna's eyes as Steele kept talking. He needed to get a handle on this, knowing how close Anna and Adria were, but surprisingly she agreed. What was up with that?

"Just don't do anything stupid, Steele. She's my best friend and has already been through seven levels of hell. I don't want her hurt."

"Chase is going to look into her financials and background. I'm not checking her out to marry the woman. Fuck."

"Yeah, you say that now. Anyway, who's going to help me bring out the rest of the food?"

They followed her into the house, then grabbed a dish and brought it out to the patio.

"Does Ethan cook for you?"

"Nope, but he has brought food into the station. Not often. I think he's worried they'll make him cook all the time."

"I wouldn't blame them, either."

"Cut it out. It's just food. It's not like I'm a Cordon Bleu Chef or anything."

Anna looked like she was considering it as she chewed. "How come you aren't? What made you go into the Air Force?"

"Eh, it's not worth telling."

"Why not?" Anna and Steele asked in unison. The last thing he wanted to do was share why he'd decided to get into the U.S. Air Force Academy instead of just going to a regular college like his parents wanted.

"Let's just say it was a lifelong fascination with flying and leave it at that." He thought Anna was going to press him further, but thankfully she dropped it. Maybe her intuition told her it wasn't a subject he wanted to discuss, at least not right then. Steele was staring at him, and he hated when his friend got that look, it meant he would find out no matter what. It was great when dealing with suspects but sucked donkey balls when it was directed toward him.

"What's our plan of action?" Anna looked so innocent, but he knew better. The wheels were turning in that beautiful mind. But she'd helped enough. Some things were better left to the professionals.

"Our plan will be handled by professionals. You've been a huge help today." The pout started as soon as the words left his mouth, but he wasn't buying it, he knew her too well. One look at Steele said otherwise. He was like putty in her hands, and Ethan couldn't wait to see how this played out. Especially since they'd already discussed keeping her out of it.

"Aww, c'mon. They're my people. If you're going to be setting them up, I should know about it." Yup, trap set. Would Steele fall in the gaping hole she'd just dug?

"We're not going to set them up. You've been watching too many crime shows. Besides this is a small town, word tends to get around. You should know that."

"Oh, I do. Which is why I don't believe my people are involved."

"But what we discovered today says differently." Steele was earnestly trying to convince her they were the good guys. He was so focused he didn't see how well she'd played him. Maybe she should have been a cop, her analytical skills were top notch. Leaning back in his chair and taking a swig of beer, he hid his grin behind the bottle.

"What? That they were our properties? That two of my agents listed all of them? As you just said, this is a small town, there are only a couple of small independents and my company. I still don't see how it proves either one is involved."

"It doesn't. But hopefully, if we get the warrant, a phone tap will." And there it was. He'd just dropped the whole enchilada right in her lap. He hadn't even seen it coming.

"Way to go, bro. So much for keeping her out of it?" Ethan couldn't keep the gloating out of his voice. He'd fallen for her tactics too many times not to appreciate how she'd led him right where she wanted him. Hell, it only took about ten minutes too. That might be a record.

"Aww, fuck. Well played, Anna. I blame your big beautiful eyes." Steele didn't even look sorry, but he had to know Ethan was going to give him hell later, and the LT would be even more pissed when he found out. Although Ethan doubted that Anna would do anything to sabotage their investigation, there was always the chance she'd say something without thinking about it. Just like Steele.

Anna grinned, but it was obvious she was upset about the whole idea. He knew she was more worried about her friend than the old dude, and it's exactly why he hadn't wanted her to know. He didn't want to invade Adria's privacy but if the judge gave them the warrant they'd tap both her and Johnson's phones. It might be the only break they'd get on this case.

"Baby, you know you can't tell anyone about this, right?"

"Yeah, I know, but it doesn't mean I'm happy."

"I know, but we have to do what we can. You need to look at it this way, a tap could just as easily prove their innocence as their guilt. Right?"

"True. But how am I going to look at either of them in the office tomorrow? I'm not going to want to talk to Adria on the phone. Our girl talk is none of the Willow Haven Police Department's business."

Steele finally had the grace to look embarrassed, and Ethan gave him a look that said, "nice one, dude."

"I know. But you can do it. You're smart and stubborn as hell, it's part of what I love about you." He saw Steele's eyebrow arch out of the corner of his eye. He didn't care if he knew or not. Ethan would be happy to yell it from the roof, or even put it on Facebook if Anna wanted.

"I'll try. But I'm going on record here that I think it's a mistake."

"Noted. And as soon as we have information we need one way or the other we'll take off the tap. That's my promise to you."

"You know, Anna, if you're going to be in a relationship with a cop, it's part of the deal. Shit hits the fan on a regular basis, even in a small town like this. If you want to be included in their lives, it's inevitable you're going to hear things you aren't going to like, or maybe shouldn't even know.

Holding it in and shutting out their wives or husbands is what destroys a relationship."

Ethan really wished Steele would shut the fuck up and go home. Or just go home. He was right in what he'd said, but he didn't know Anna's history and reminding her that their job could be dangerous wasn't exactly going to help the situation. He dreaded Anna's reaction. He was more than relieved when she absorbed the information and didn't freak out. She was smart, beautiful and everything he never dreamed he'd find in a woman, but he also knew how skittish she was about getting hurt in love again. This was all so new, he didn't want to send her running.

Nodding as she stood up to clear away the dinner dishes, she was quiet at first. "I know, and up until now, we've had a kind of unspoken understanding that we didn't bring work home. But I guess that's all about to change. Actually, I guess it already has." Then without another word or waiting for one of them to respond she turned and went inside.

"Mother fucker. You just couldn't keep your big mouth shut, could you?"

"Fuck, bro. I know better, you know I do. But she's good. I wasn't expecting it."

"You interrogate people all the time, how the hell didn't you see what she was doing? She pegged you dead-on, it's like she had a handbook or something."

"Maybe she watches a lot of cop shows?"

Ethan rolled his eyes, but that was better than punching Steele. He didn't even realize he was opening and closing his fist until he looked down, and that wasn't a good sign. "You just made this a thousand times harder for her. You do realize that, right?"

"Yeah, I'm starting to."

"Adria is her best friend, maybe her only friend. All she does is work. Besides Tag, his girlfriend, Mac, and his wife, Adria is it. And you just made it, so she's going to have trouble looking her in the face."

"Well, she's got you too. But I get it. So why didn't you stop me?"

"Would it have done any good? Other than me telling you to shut the fuck up, which would have made it even worse, what the hell was I supposed to do. Deck you?"

"You didn't look too upset at the time."

"True, I was enjoying it—maybe too much. But of all things, Mr. King of Interrogation, you just walked into a big ass sink hole. Amateur, dude."

Steele ran his hand through his hair making it stand on end, a sure sign he was as agitated as

Ethan. "What if you lie and tell her we can't get the warrant?"

"Lie to me? Are you serious? And I was starting to like you." Anna stood in the open doorway and looked like she was about to explode. The storm clouds in her eyes caught Steele by surprise. Damn, he was getting the full Anna, but he had no one to blame but himself.

"He didn't mean it, baby. Besides, I wouldn't lie to you. You should know me better." His words seemed to defuse some of her irritation, but if looks could kill, Steele would be in need of an ambulance right about then.

"I'm sorry, Anna. It was only a suggestion to make it easier. But you're right it was stupid. On that note, I think I'm going to go home before I make things any worse. Thank you for dinner and the company. I had a great time until I stuck my size thirteens in my mouth."

"Probably a good idea. I'll see you at the station in the morning."

"I really am sorry, Anna."

To her credit, she didn't throw anything at Steele. "It's okay. I'm on edge too. I probably shouldn't have worked you so hard for information I didn't want or need to know. I'll take half the blame."

Steele smiled in relief and bravely gave her a hug as he made his way into the house. "Next time will be better, I promise."

"I'm sure it will. No work next time at all."

"Deal."

"I'll walk you out." Ethan grabbed her hand and squeezed it as he followed Steele into the house, and she gave him a half smile.

CHAPTER SIX

After Steele had left, Ethan helped her clean the kitchen and put everything away. He was dropping hints like little land mines hoping she'd invite him to stay the night again. But she was going to disappoint him. Anna's Sundays were spent preparing for the work week. That meant updating her schedule and planner, sorting through bills, checking all the latest listings from the weekend to share at the morning meeting. Her day always ended with yoga and a shower.

Instead, she'd spent her Sunday helping Willow Haven's sexiest detective and his partner, and making herself crazy with worry. It wasn't until Steele left that she remembered the possible stalker creepy guy who might have been following her on Saturday. Considering how freaked out it had her at the time, she couldn't believe she'd forgotten about it until then.

She should probably tell Ethan now that she knew about the robberies. He had been hanging around the house, the same one that had the break-in. Anna didn't believe in coincidences, and this was just too odd to ignore. Seeing the open wine bottle, she was tempted to pour another glass, but it probably wasn't the best idea. Not with work tomorrow and so much going on.

"Do you want some coffee?"

"Always. I'll make it," Ethan said as he grabbed the teapot and filled it with water. While he did that, she ground the beans and put them in the French press. Once the water was near boiling, they added it to the pot and carried everything out to the patio. The sun was just setting, and it was the perfect summer evening, even if her insides were in turmoil.

Passing Ethan his black coffee, she added sugar and half-and-half to hers before reclining in one of the chaise lounges. It was so peaceful. She sighed with pleasure that she wished she could hold on to just a little longer before she had to open the can of worms.

"What's wrong, sweetheart? I don't know if you realize it, but whatever is going on in that head of yours is broadcast all over your beautiful face. Don't bother trying to say it's nothing."

The immature Anna wanted to stick out her tongue and say, "bite me." But she had to be an adult, and that meant coming clean. "Something weird happened after the open house on Saturday." Yup, that got his attention.

"And you're just telling me now?"

"With everything going on it kind of slipped my mind. I got home and smelled your amazing dinner, and all I could think about was food."

"Umm, sure. Nope, not buying it. What weird thing happened?"

"Well..." She hesitated and took another sip of coffee as she searched for the right words. The last thing she wanted was for him to freak out and decide she wasn't safe. "I'm sure it was nothing."

"If it worried you then it's probably something. Gut instincts are usually right."

He was right, it had freaked her out and just because she didn't want it to be true didn't mean it wasn't. "When I closed up the open house on Saturday, there was a guy leaning against a rusted green pickup truck and smoking. I don't remember ever seeing him before, and he kind of gave me the creeps."

"Can you describe him?"

"Probably, it wasn't dark yet. He was wearing sunglasses, but I got a pretty good look at his face."

"Good. Anything else?"

"Yeah. Umm..." He was going to be pissed, so pissed. Why hadn't she realized it before? *Because you're too stubborn for your own good, that's why.* He put his coffee cup on the table and crossed his arms like he knew he wasn't going to like what was coming next.

"Outside the open house wasn't the only time I saw him."

"What? Dammit. After everything we've been talking about today, you're making me drag this out of you now? You really need to work on your trust issues, sweetheart."

"I know. But when I got home and didn't see him following me, I figured it was all in my imagination."

"Even if it was, you should have told me. If not right away, then definitely after you heard about the robberies."

He was right, and she had no excuse other than she'd honestly forgotten until then. With everything else going on, it had been the furthest thing from her mind. "It was stupid, yes, I realize that now, but I really did forget."

"Well, there's nothing we can do about it now. For all we know, he's the one planning the robberies. Or maybe he's stalking you. Either way, we need to take care of it as soon as possible. Please promise me you won't hold back any more information whether you think it's pertinent or not."

"I promise."

"Good." He softened his tone now that she'd agreed to do what he wanted, but she didn't care. In this instance, he was right, and she was wrong. She was woman enough to admit it. "Where else did you see him?"

"At the office. Not at first but the truck was there when I was leaving to come home. At least, I think it was the same truck. I couldn't see the guy, just the glow of his cigarette through the tinted window. At first, I didn't think anyone was in there until I tried to drive by to get the license plate. I only got the first two letters before he took off in a hurry."

"Good instincts but dangerous, especially because we don't know why he's following you."

"We don't really know that he *is* following me either. He might have been there for some other reason.

The look he gave her was classic and would have made her parents proud. It was the typical 'are you shitting me, do you need to be punished' look, and he wore it well. She struggled to keep the grin off her face. He wouldn't have taken that well.

Ethan pulled out his phone and tapped a text to someone, she was sure it was to Steele. "What were the two letters you saw?"

"An S and an R. It was the regular sunshine state plate too."

"Okay. Did you recognize the make or model of the truck?"

"No, sorry. Just that it was green, old, rusty and looked like it was on its last leg, except for the tinted windows. Now that I think about it, that's kind of weird."

"Very. I know you're always too busy for much of anything, but do you think you could come by the station at some point tomorrow and work with a sketch artist?"

"No promises, but I'll try. It might be late; you know like after work."

"That's fine, but I really would like to get that sketch circulated as soon as possible." He typed some more and then slid the phone back into his pocket. Apparently, it was police business, and it wasn't going to be shared.

"Maybe I'll be able to stop by before I go in. I'll have to see how much I get done tonight."

"What do you have to do tonight?"

"My usual prep for the week, schedules, plans, new listing information, bills, the usual stuff. Then I usually do some yoga, shower, and go to bed."

Shaking his head, he had a weird expression on his face. "Do you ever just have down time where you don't do a damn thing? You know, be spontaneous?"

"Well yeah of course I do." Did she? Now that she thought about it, maybe she didn't. Her schedule had worked for her, until now anyway. Kept her busy and focused on the end game. But now all of that had changed once she'd let Ethan into her life. If she hadn't had blinders on, she would have realized it a whole lot sooner.

"So, is this your way of saying you want me to go home so you can get your stuff done?"

Did she want that? Just a bit ago she was ready to show him the door, but now after telling him about Mr. Creepy Pants, she would rather he stayed.

***

He had to fight the urge to strangle her, not really. But dammit, why hadn't she told him? He wanted to go off on a rant, but he knew better. She would have closed up like a night-blooming jasmine in the morning, and that would have been that. But he'd kept his cool. Fuck. He deserved a freaking Oscar for that performance. Now he was just waiting to see if she wanted him to stay or not. With all of her "excuses," he figured any minute she was going to ask him to go home. Not that he could blame her either, she'd had a hell of a weekend, and he still didn't have any clothes or toiletries. On the other hand, he didn't want to leave her alone in this house, alarm or not. She carried his heart, and he would give up his life to protect her, whether she fully realized it or not.

"It's been great having you here, but I do think I need some time to myself to wrap my head around everything. I know you think I'm not safe, but I am. I will set the alarm as soon as you walk out the door, you can even double check all the doors and windows before you leave."

She was trying to placate him, but it wasn't working. Until he knew more about the dirt bag who'd been following her, he wanted her under his protection. "Are you sure you won't feel safer if I stay? And there's the bonus nookie-time."

"I know what you're doing, honey, I do. But I really think I need some time to myself before I have to take off running for another week. I promise I'll come by the station at some point tomorrow to work with the sketch artist, I'll keep the phone by the bed with your number primed for the call. I'll be safe and careful."

She was stubborn but so was he, and this was one time he wasn't backing down. He was not leaving his woman alone even if it meant he'd be sleeping in his car in her driveway. "I don't doubt that you believe that. But I'm not going to give in on this. Until we know more about this guy, I don't want you to be alone."

"But…"

"Nope. If I have to, I'll stay in my car, but I'm not leaving the grounds." She crossed her arms, and the storm clouds were back in her eyes, but he didn't care. He was waiting for the explosion, but instead, the storm passed.

"You'd really do that for me? Sleep in your car?"

"Of course. How many different ways do I need to show you how much I love you before you start to believe it? Has no one in your life ever put your well-being first?" He expected a quick retort, but tears welled in her eyes, hovered on her lower lids and threatened to fall.

The tears were his undoing. Before she could say another word, he was on his knees next to her chair and pulling her into his arms. She didn't make a sound just tucked her head under his chin. He wouldn't even have known she was crying except his t-shirt got wet from her tears. He rocked her and let her cry, and he wondered how long she'd held it in.

Lynne St. James

Chapter Seven

Monday morning arrived way too early. Usually, Anna woke refreshed and ready to tackle the new week, this morning not so much. For the first time in forever, she hadn't done her prep work for the week. Instead, she cried herself a river in Ethan's arms before he led her to the bedroom and made love to her most of the night. She'd never felt so loved and cherished in her entire life. But she was paying the price this morning. There wasn't going to be enough coffee on the planet to make her perky.

"We're agreed, right? You're going to be hyper-vigilant until we catch this guy. Any sign of him or the truck and you're going to call me. Or Steele if you can't reach me. Which won't happen. Oh, and I programmed Steele's number into your phone."

"Yes, boss," she answered with a yawn. Two cups of coffee down and they'd had no effect whatsoever. Ethan smacked her on the butt as he grabbed an apple and then dropped a kiss on her lips.

"I mean it, baby. No risks is your motto. Got it?"

"Yeah, yeah. And what about your motto? You take more risks than I ever have."

"I'm a man. I'm equipped." That was ballsy, but she knew he was trying to lighten the mood, and it worked. She laughed and tossed a banana at his head.

"Hey, that's gonna leave a bruise."

"Awww, did I hurt the big bad police detective?" She knew she was in trouble before the sound of her words dissipated. Ethan grabbed her by the waist and swung her around so fast she thought her coffee was going make a speedy return.

"If we had more time, I'd show you just how big and bad I am. Although, after last night, I am surprised you need a reminder." The mischief in his eyes should have warned her, but she was either too slow or too tired, and next thing she knew she was laying on the kitchen island, and he'd lifted her shirt and blew raspberries on her stomach. Then he stood her on the floor, kissed her soundly and was gone.

"Holy crap. That man is full of surprises."

"I heard that, and don't you forget it," he called from the front room before she heard the click of the door closing. Then the alarm dinged when the door was reopened. "And don't forget to set the alarm. Later, my sex goddess."

After he was gone, the house was way too quiet. It seemed like every time he left, whether he was there for ten minutes or in this case almost thirty-six hours, he took all the happiness with him. Was her life really that dull? Had she let all the happiness drain away to keep herself insulated from hurt? It sure seemed like it, and she was more than ready to live again. Exhaustion be damned, today was the first day of the rest of her life, even if it meant lots of stress and worry, it was okay. She felt alive, really alive for the first time in years.

It didn't look like she'd have time to stop by the police station before work, Ethan would just have to get over it. She'd see if she could make it at lunch or after work it would have to be. Monday's were usually her busiest days, and she'd be swimming upstream all day.

Instead of being the first one in, she was the last one in to work. Greeting everyone as she headed into her office she smiled at the look of surprise on their faces. She had a half hour before the Monday morning staff meeting, and a shitload of listings to go through, or not. Maybe it was time to start delegating. It's not like it was complicated. That decided, she opened their in-house program, and she checked the status of everyone's listings. Two sales on Saturday, excellent. Noting the information to discuss at the meeting, she still needed to figure out what if anything she was going to say about the rash of break-ins. Chances were if she'd seen it on the news so had at least a few of her employees.

A knock at her door distracted her train of thought. "Morning, Anna. You looked like you could use this," Jenny said as she put a steaming mug of coffee on her desk.

"Oh yeah. Thank you."

"You're welcome. How'd the open house go?"

"We had a lot of traffic, I think Adria might have a sale this week, well except..." her voice trailed off when she remembered the robbery. Had they trashed the house? Was it even sellable at this point? Ethan said they usually didn't damage anything in the house, but still, it was a crime scene. Would anyone want to buy it now?

"What's wrong?" Jenny's face showed concern, but there was something else in her expression too, something Anna couldn't quite place. Maybe she'd heard the news and was waiting to see if Anna would say anything?

"I didn't get a lot of sleep last night. I think I'm just a little slow today," Anna said with a laugh.

"Too much weekend. Or maybe I should say, too much Ethan in your weekend?"

"Maybe." Anna grinned, it wasn't out of character for her and Jenny to discuss any of this, but after Ethan's warning, she second guessed everything. "How about you? Did anything come up while I was out?"

"Nope, it was all quiet. I think the weather was just too nice to spend the weekend inside. I hung out with some friends, ate pizza, drank beer, and just chilled. It was good."

"Sounds like it. Good for you. There's a lot to be said for relaxing."

"What kept you at home?" Adria said from the doorway.

"I think that's my cue, meeting in ten."

"Thanks." Was there something off with Jenny today or was it just Anna being "hyper-vigilant" for weirdness? Ethan was going to turn her into a paranoid mess before this was through. "I might have had a house guest," she said after Jenny closed her office door.

"No way! Ethan stayed over? Hot damn. It's about time."

"Actually, he stayed Saturday night too."

"Holy crap, woman. When you finally give in you really go for it."

Anna laughed. Yeah, she guessed she did and that part of the weekend was amazing. Then she remembered Ethan and Steele would be trying to get warrants for the phone taps and some of the sunshine of her morning dimmed. "I guess I did or do. Depending on how you look at it," she said with a forced smile. But Adria was so excited for her Anna didn't think she noticed. She was going to have to tread carefully today, being extra tired was going to make it more difficult not to slip.

"I want details. I have to live vicariously through you."

"No, you don't, you're just even more stubborn than I am."

"But Scotty..."

"Don't use Scotty as an excuse. He's in junior high now, do you think he wants to have to worry about his mom when he'd rather be hanging with his buds? You're just scared, and trust me I know all about scared."

Adria sighed and leaned back in the chair. "Maybe, but..."

"No buts allowed, and I think I found the perfect guy for you."

"Oh God, no. No blind dates."

"You'd be missing out if you couldn't see him. He's hotter than..."

"Who is?" Ethan said as he opened the door to her office.

"Doesn't anyone knock anymore? Damn. And none of your business."

"You must be talking about me then," he said smugly. Adria laughed.

"I think we need to pick this up later. How about I pick up lunch, and we eat in today?"

Anna glanced at Ethan and saw the slight shake of his head. Damn, he was going to press her to go see the sketch artist. "Umm…"

Ethan cut her off, while she tried to figure out how to respond. "Actually, I called dibs on lunch first thing this morning. But tomorrow she's all yours."

"Oh, I see how I rate. Gotcha," Adria said but couldn't hold her straight face. "See you at the meeting. Bye, Ethan. Have a nice lunch with my best friend."

"What's up? I have a meeting."

"I wanted to make sure you got in okay."

"Unless I'm wrong, you have a phone with text messaging that works just fine." The look on Ethan's face proved she was right, he had an ulterior motive for being there.

"I was hoping you'd let me talk to your staff at the meeting. Steele and I think that stirring the pot might help trigger a response if one of your employees is involved."

"That might not be such a bad idea. Does that mean you didn't get the warrant?"

"We don't know yet. Oh, and Steele is here too."

"Is he here for the meeting or to dig up dirt on my employees?"

"Relax, we're not going to cause trouble—yet. But if something or someone doesn't seem right all bets are off."

"Do I have a choice?"

"Of course you do. We can't force you to help us, but I'd think you'd want to know as much as we do. Especially if all your people are innocent, then they're in danger too if it escalates. We've been lucky so far that no one's been hurt or worse."

She'd thought that herself, and he had a point. "Okay. Let's go, it's meeting time."

***

He'd taken a chance showing up, but Ethan hadn't wanted to give her a chance to say no. After what she'd told him about the guy watching her, he was more convinced than ever that someone in her office was involved. And he wanted to close this case as soon as possible before it got any worse.

When they'd told the LT everything, they'd found out he called the DA himself and asked him to get them a warrant, but he hadn't lied either. He didn't know if they'd been successful or not in getting one. Until then, he and Steele were going to work every angle they could. That meant showing up at Anna's office and hijacking her staff meeting.

They decided Ethan would do the talking and Steele would use his keen sense of observation on everyone in the room, his words not Ethan's. It was as good a plan as any. When everyone was gathered, he explained about the robberies, and what they needed to do to make sure they stayed safe. They were recommending that no agent go out alone until the culprits were caught.

A low rumbling in the room let him know they didn't like the idea. He understood they were in competition and worked on commission, but there was money, and there was safety, and most if not all of Anna's employees were probably innocent. Although, he really liked Hugh Johnson for it, even if he didn't seem like the brainiac type.

"I'm going to leave our cards at the front desk with Jenny. If any of you see anything suspicious, or you think of anything that can help us try to catch these guys, give either myself or Steele a call. It's imperative that you all are careful until we catch these guys. So far no one's been hurt, and we don't want that to change."

He leaned against one of the walls as Anna finished her meeting, going over the sales stats and delegating some work. He couldn't have been happier to hear that either. It meant she was going to ease up, and that was a plus as far as he was concerned.

After the meeting, he and Steele talked to Anna for a bit before they headed back to the station. She'd agreed to come over and work with the sketch artist, he told her she'd be rewarded with another of Dixie's roast beef sandwiches, and he'd been rewarded with a million-dollar smile. All in all, even though he was worried about her and the case, he couldn't remember when he'd been happier.

A few hours later she was sitting with the sketch artist at the station. It turned out she remembered more details than he'd expected and the sketch turned out well. Lunch went well until Rob Martin, the assistant DA, showed up with the warrant. Apparently, the judge wanted this cleared up quickly since it was an election year and both he and the DA were up for reelection. Gotta love politics.

Anna wasn't happy, but she'd accepted that they needed to do anything in their power to solve the case. He reminded her to watch for anything suspicious with any of her employees, not just Hugh or even Adria. They were all suspects until they weren't at this point. Before she went back to her office, he pulled her into the breakroom.

"I'm really sorry you have to deal with all of this, baby."

"Me too, but it'll work out, right?"

"Of course, we always get our man," he said with a laugh and false bravado. There wasn't a lot of high crime in Willow Haven, mostly minor drug busts, stolen cars and shoplifting were the majority of his cases.

She looked tired, and it was his fault, but he wasn't one bit sorry. Every minute he'd spent loving on her last night had been magic. Which reminded him. "Are we staying at your place again or mine tonight?"

"What?"

"Did you forget what I said last night? I'm not going to leave you alone until we catch this guy or figure out what's going on."

"Aren't you overreacting a bit?"

"Nope, I'm not. Besides, nothing I do to protect you would ever be too much."

"Damn, you're tough. Fine. My place is bigger and has a better kitchen, so you come over."

"You got it. We can go out for dinner, or I can cook."

"I'll let you know when I have a better idea how late I'll have to work tonight."

"Okay, that works. Text me when you get back to the office." He slid a finger along her cheek and under her chin, tilting her face up to his to kiss her. He hadn't intended to do anything but give her a light kiss, but she was a witch, and all it took was one small touch to set him off. Only when Steele came looking for him did he break off the kiss. As he stepped back, he caught the dreamy expression in her molten-chocolate eyes, and he had to hold himself back from going all Tarzan.

"Um, the LT is looking for you," Steele said after clearing his throat to let them know he was there.

"Okay."

"I need to get back to the office. I'll see you later."

"Don't forget to let me know you got back."

"Yes, dad," Anna replied as she shook her head.

"Bye, Anna."

"Bye, Steele. Do some real work, will you?"

Chapter Eight

After Anna had returned to her office, Ethan and Steele took a ride over to the Eagle Security and Protection Agency. While they were having lunch, Chase sent a text to Steele letting him know they had some information for them.

Ethan had met Chase and some of the other guys from ESP a few times at Steele's place, but he didn't know them well, and he'd never been to their offices. But he was impressed when they walked in. It rivaled anything he'd come across at Air Force Command, and the command center was top notch.

The team at ESP were all ex-military, either just retired or disabled. Chase had been trying to get Steele to come on board since he'd come to Florida. Their set up was intriguing, but it didn't interest Ethan at least not now. He didn't want to be traveling the globe anymore, he was happy to be stuck in Willow Haven with Anna. Being on assignment who knows where and when was not the life for a married man, and he hoped that would be where his relationship with Anna was headed.

Although, unlike the military at least their missions weren't secret, but they could still be dangerous.

After giving them the tour, they sat down in the command center and Chase's computer whiz-kid, Rock, went over all the information. Rock was his SEAL name, but he'd kept it unlike most of the others. Steele said Chase's name was Frost when he was part of the Teams. But Rock, well he looked more like a mountain, tall didn't sum it up, the man had to be close to seven foot, and looked like he could take down a whole football team by himself. Not a man you wanted to piss off. Looking at him you'd think he was a boxer or something, but finding out that his best "skills" were with computers was surprising. Just proves you that you shouldn't judge a book by its cover.

"Apparently, one of her employees—Hugh Johnson—has a gambling problem, one is cheating on his wife, another is mortgaged out the wazoo to put his kids through college, then there's Adria, I know you were worried about her. She looks pretty clean though, she has her widow pay from the military, but she's been socking it away for her kid's education it looks like. She doesn't have any extra income other than her paycheck. There were a few others with a couple of questionable things in their backgrounds but nothing that would indicate what you're looking for. I'd say your best bet is the Johnson guy."

"That's what we were thinking too. But so far, we don't have any proof. We finally got a warrant for his phone, but nothing has turned up yet. Did your digging come up with anything else?"

Chase shrugged and nodded to Rock. What had they been holding back? And why?

"It looks like Anna Taggart has been taking out some pretty big withdrawals in cash lately. Not sure what she's doing with it, but it's big money. Each time it's cash and just under the ten-grand number that would trigger the feds."

"What? Who told you to look into Anna?" Ethan looked around the room, and his eyes rested on Steele. Of course. Who else. "Why? You know damn well she's not a suspect."

"I know, but while we were looking, I wanted to make sure."

"What do you mean? I was freakin' with her during the last break-in."

"Not really. Remember she got home just after you got the call from LT."

Shit, Steele was right, but he also knew Anna was clean. He knew it with every fiber of his being. There's no way she'd be involved in this, there had to be a good explanation for where the money was going. "You still had no right. Or you should have at least told me."

"I'm sorry. But I knew you'd never go for it, and I had to look out for you."

"Listen, Ethan, I know you're not happy about this. But Steele had a point. You can't just eliminate suspects because your gut tells you to. And no, she doesn't look good for the robberies, but something is definitely up. What the hell is she doing with all that money? It's close to one hundred grand, that's not chump change. Maybe someone's blackmailing her, or maybe she's up to something. Either way, I don't think it hurts to dig a little deeper into her and the rest of the company."

Pain sliced through Ethan's head at that thought of invading Anna's privacy this way, but Chase and Steele had a point. Something was up, and she hadn't mentioned it at all. No one takes large sums of cash out of the bank the way she has without a good reason. "Go ahead, but keep it quiet. I don't want her getting wind of this. This is my woman, and I know there's a good reason for this. We just don't know what it is yet."

"I sure hope so."

So did Ethan. The information on Johnson was good, but Anna? That was a whole other ballgame. No wonder they wanted them to come down to the office to talk about it. He was ever happier that only the four of them knew about the investigation. She'd be mortified if she found out this was going on, and he knew she'd end it. And honestly, could he blame her?

***

It took everything he had not to ask Anna about the money when they got back to her house that evening. He knew there had to be a good explanation, but for the life of him he couldn't figure it out. But with everything else going on the last thing he wanted to do was confront her about suspicions. She hadn't even admitted to loving him yet, and for him to accuse her of anything would put an end to it.

It made for strained conversation while they ate the homemade pizza he'd prepared. Working the dough helped drive out some of the tension riding him since they'd left the ESP offices. He'd been so pissed at Steele he couldn't even look at him. But after listening to his partner justify it on the ride back to the station, he knew he was right. They needed to look under every stone no matter who the individuals were or their relationship. But just because he understood and agreed didn't mean he had to like it.

Anna didn't get home until after seven, and he was getting ready to text her when she walked in the door. "Hi, sexy detective, I'm home. Did you miss me?"

"Sure did. How was the rest of your day?"

"Great, okay, not so much. I was worried I would say something I shouldn't every time I had to talk to someone. I pretty much hid out in my office doing paperwork most of the afternoon. I'm sure Adria thinks I'm upset with her by now."

"Why? You were talking to her this morning when I got there."

"Yeah but I haven't called her or sat with her in her office or anything since the meeting. Usually, we have coffee in the afternoon and unwind before she goes home."

"I'm sorry. You know you don't have to act differently with her. Right? Why don't you give her a call after dinner?"

"I would, but knowing it's being recorded...no thank you. And sorry, even if you're sitting here listening to the other side of the conversation it's different than knowing someone is recording every word."

"I'm sorry, baby. But hopefully this will all be over soon, and you can go back to normal. Then you can tell her whatever you want."

"I hope so. Did you make any headway today? Figure out who the real suspects are yet?"

"We're working on it, but so far we still don't have much to go on. We are working a few leads."

"But you can't tell me, right?"

"Right. I would, but then I'd have to kill you. And you know, just don't think I could find another Anna to love like I love you." His words had the intended effect, and she smiled. The first smile since they'd sat down to dinner.

"Got it. I don't really feel like dying yet either. I have a few bucket list items still to cross off."

"Oh really? Care to share?"

"Nope. You won't share, I won't share."

"That's not fair. This is work."

"I know. But I have to keep you guessing about some things, right?" If she only knew just how much he was wondering about he doubted she'd be so flippant. But he had to keep telling himself that he knew this woman, loved this woman, and he knew better than to think she'd be involved in anything illegal.

"So that's how we're going to play this huh?"

"Yup. I think so." She batted her long eyelashes at him and tried to play the innocent card, but he knew better. Her cheeks were already a lovely rosy shade of pink. He loved how she wasn't afraid to let him see she wanted him. Even with all the other stuff going on.

"C'mere, wench. I think it's time to teach you a lesson."

"What? Oh no, you don't. Ethan Price, don't you dare." But it was too late, he'd already walked around the table and picked her up and put her over his shoulder. Then he gave her one smack on the butt for good measure as he took her onto the patio.

She must have figured out where they were going and she started to struggle for real. But he wasn't letting go. He'd wanted to make love to her in the pool since the first time he'd been in her backyard, and they both needed to get rid of all the built-up tension of the day.

"Ethan, put me down now. I told you, I don't like to be carried."

"I will just give me another minute or two. I hope that dress wasn't expensive."

"What?"

"The dress, was it expensive?"

"Umm, what? Oh no, you don't. Don't even think about it. Ethan, put me down now!"

"You want down? My pleasure, baby." And walked them both into the pool. When he'd gotten to her place he'd changed into shorts and a t-shirt, but she was still in her work clothes. He'd probably have to buy her a new dress, but it was so going to be worth it.

"Oh my God, I can't believe you..." He cut her off with the kiss he'd been holding back since lunch. This time there was no restraint, he licked and nibbled on her lips then demanded entrance into her mouth with his tongue. He needed her, all of her, and he couldn't wait.

By the time he pulled back from their kiss, her face was flushed, and she was limp in his arms. Her eyes fluttered open and flashed emerald fire in molten-chocolate. Her words were barely audible and came out more like a sigh.

"I want you."

"Baby, I never stop wanting you." He pulled off his t-shirt and kicked off his shorts exposing his huge erection. They were waist deep in the water, and he slid her down the front of him until she stood in front of him. Her eyes never left his. His hands sought the zipper on the back of her dress, and as lowered it, she dipped her shoulders, so the soaked dress slid down exposing her satin bra. Ethan couldn't remember when she looked sexier, standing in the water, her long dark hair spread out over her shoulders, he lips swollen from his kisses. Like a mermaid, she looked exotic and sexy, and he needed to sink deep inside her.

After removing the dress, he opened her bra and tossed it onto the pool deck, then her matching panties. They were both panting with desire and pent up emotion, almost desperate for each other.

This time wouldn't be gentle, and he prayed he wouldn't hurt her. But she was ready for him, and he slid into her like she was made for him. Her muscles gripped him and tried to hold on has he started slowly but soon built up the pounding rhythm they both needed. He wrapped her legs around his hips as he drove deep. Thrusting over and over again while his tongue swept her mouth, taking all she had to offer.

Her nails dug deep into the skin of his shoulders, as she clung to him. She broke their kiss as she orgasmed, clenching so tightly around him she pushed him over the edge.

Making love to her in the water was even more intense than he'd expected. But now he wished they were someplace soft and flat where he could cuddle her and show her just how much he cherished her. Instead, he moved them over to the waterfall and like something out of a tropical paradise he rinsed her hair under the water, and with water drops sparkling on her eyelashes she looked like a sea goddess in his arms.

"I love you, Anna. The words don't even come close to how I feel, but they're all I have. But I will spend the rest of my life showing you how much you mean to me if you'll let me." He knew what he was doing, it was as close to a proposal as he'd ever gotten in his life, and he had no idea how she'd respond. But at that moment it felt right, and the words had a mind of their own.

"Oh, Ethan. You are amazing."

Not what he was hoping for, but he'd take it. The words she hadn't said shone in her eyes as clear as the water they were floating in. He would wait, and when she finally uttered those words he was so desperate to hear, he'd be in paradise.

Lynne St. James

Chapter Nine

Monday became Tuesday and then Wednesday and soon the entire week had passed, and they'd fallen into a routine. Anna was surprised how quickly she got used to having Ethan around. As much as she wanted him to solve the case, it would mean he wouldn't have to stay with her. That would also mean she wouldn't have him in her bed, in her arms, and wake up in the morning snuggled in to his side. And that didn't even include the excellent meals he'd been making every night and sharing coffee in the morning. There was something to be said for sharing her home with him.

She had a decision to make about their future living arrangements. As much as she loved having him there, she still hesitated about making it permanent. That frisson of fear she couldn't shake, that something would happen to him and she'd lose him like she lost Ryan. She didn't know how she'd recover a second time from that kind of a heartbreak.

The thought of only seeing Ethan on the weekends and maybe one night during the week made her sad to think about. Having him there had made her feel safer and cherished. She didn't doubt Ethan's love for her at all, even though she hadn't been able to bring herself to say the words to him. In her heart, she knew she loved him, maybe more than she'd loved anyone. But to say the words out loud scared the crap out of her. And there was the rub. If she couldn't tell him, was she ready to take the next step in their relationship?

Ethan and Steele were both disappointed that their visit to her meeting hadn't turned up anything. She knew they had more information then they could share, but still, as the days went on her tension eased in the office as it looked like her employees would be cleared. Anna wanted to tell them 'I told you so,' but she still had a niggling feeling she was missing something. She also hadn't seen Mr. Creepy Pants again, but she could have sworn she'd caught the truck in her rearview mirror one or two times. She was a good girl too; she'd told Ethan as soon as she'd gotten home. It was too bad Florida didn't require front license plates, or she might have had a chance to get more than just the first two letters.

The week flew by, and they still hadn't solved the case. Now it was Saturday again. Would there be another break-in? Or had Ethan's investigation scared them off? Hoping for a nice quiet evening, they decided to stay home, order pizza and watch the movie *Deadpool*. Unfortunately, their luck didn't hold out. The phone rang at eleven-thirty. Anna was half asleep leaning against Ethan, but the ringing was like an instant 'On' button.

"Damn."

"I know. I was hoping, too." It was Steele, he'd gotten the call first and was passing on the news which wasn't all that good. Again, it was a Willow Haven Realty listing that had been hit. That much she'd figured out from listening to Ethan's half of the conversation, but the look on his face scared her. An ominous feeling turned the pizza and beer in her stomach into a roiling bucket of acid.

"Got it. I'll be there in about ten minutes. I don't have to tell you if the press shows up we have no comment, right? Did someone contact his wife? Okay.

Contact his wife? It didn't sound good. What horrible thing had happened now? Had one of their clients been home? But why would the wife have to be notified then?

Ethan disconnected the call and when his eyes met hers she knew. She wasn't sure how she did, but she knew.

"It's Hugh, isn't it?"

"I'm afraid so. Did he have an open house today?"

"Yeah, I think so."

"Apparently, he didn't bring a 'buddy,' and his wife called the station when he didn't come home for dinner and didn't answer his phone. It was too soon for her to file a missing persons' report, but given the circumstances, they'd decided to check it out. Before they could send a unit to his house, they got a call from one of the neighbors who had just returned from the movies. The lights were on, and the front door was wide open."

Dizziness hit her like a wave, and if she hadn't been sitting, she'd probably have fallen over. "Why was he there alone?"

"That's what I'd like to know. Did you assign partners or leave it up to them?"

"I left it up to them, but they were supposed to tell Jenny so she could keep track of everything."

"Good. If he followed the rules, then we should know who was supposed to be with him." Words wouldn't form, so she nodded. Hugh Johnson was dead? It didn't seem possible, she'd seen him earlier in the day, and he was as obnoxious as always, but that was him. It had been for as long as she'd know him. Poor Betty. They'd been married forever; all their kids were grown and gone. She would be devastated.

"I should probably go over and see Betty." When he looked at her oddly, she clarified. "Hugh's wife, umm widow now. I guess. She's the sweetest thing, and the opposite of her husband."

"I'd rather you didn't. At least not until someone can go with you. He was murdered, and we don't know who's behind it. I'd prefer you stay here and set the alarm as soon as I close the door."

Anna understood his reasoning, but she wasn't a child. She was trained in self-defense and was more than capable of taking care of herself, whether he wanted to admit it or not.

He got ready and headed out. She knew he waited outside until he was sure she'd set the alarm. She watched him drive away then got dressed. Yes, he was worried about her, but this was getting out of hand. If she didn't put her foot down soon, he'd have her wrapped in cotton so she didn't break, and to use one of his expressions, "fuck that noise."

Double-checking the address, she left a note on the kitchen counter for Ethan in case he returned before she did. She disabled the alarm, went through the mudroom, and opened the garage. As she stepped into the garage, she was hit hard on the back of her head.

***

Ethan arrived at the house as CSU finished and released the scene. Steele was conferring with the LT, and there were several uniforms spread out to keep the press and public away. It was exactly the scenario they'd been hoping to avoid. Hugh's violent death brought back visions of Iraq, but he pushed them away. He needed to stay focused on the scene.

Steele waved him over, and his grim look didn't bode well. "What do we know?"

"Not much yet. CSU dusted for prints, but from what the coroner said, the victim was killed with blunt force trauma. It looked like he fought back. But we still don't know whether it is more than one person. It's not like the victim was in the best shape or young. He was sixty-five according to his driver's license."

Ethan nodded. It wouldn't have taken too much to subdue him so it could have been one man, although he was convinced it was a group. They got in and out too efficiently for it to be only one.

"We'll know more when we get the autopsy report but don't look for that until Monday," Lt. Mark Watson stated. It wasn't often he came to a crime scene anymore, so the fact that he was there meant it had gone all the way up the food chain, and no one was happy.

"Did the coroner say anything else?"

"No, liver temp indicated the victim had been deceased about four hours. It was still light when it went down. I'd say that pretty much cements your theory that they really know the neighborhoods they're hitting."

"Exactly."

"Does Anna know?" Steele asked after their lieutenant walked away to speak to the press.

"Yeah. She wanted to go see his widow, but I told her to stay home until I had more information."

"You *told* her? You really don't listen, do you? No wonder you've been single for so long. You don't *tell* a woman like Anna what to do. You ask her or cajole her. But anything remotely like an order will only get you the opposite of what you want."

Ethan looked at the house, crawling with police, then back to Steele. Was he right? He pulled his phone from his pocket and dialed her cell. He didn't want to wait for her to text him back. Except she wasn't answering. One ring, two, three, four, voicemail. *What the fuck?*

"She's not answering, is she? What did I tell you! You really do need to get on Facebook more."

"So, you're telling me the handbook on how to deal with women is stalking Facebook?"

"Yup. Just do it, you'll see."

"First, I have to find my woman. She was half-asleep when I left so maybe she went to bed and didn't hear the phone."

"Really? That's the best you've got? Bro, what have you been smoking?"

Ethan rolled his eyes. Sometimes he thought Steele would have been better as a private investigator, or maybe he should have joined his brother's security firm.

Calling over one of the uniforms, he asked him to go to Anna's house and let him know what he found. He'd have gone himself, but he had a crime to investigate.

They went into the house after putting on their gloves and crime scene booties. The place was trashed. It was a huge departure from the other crime scenes. Those homes hadn't been wrecked inside, just cleaned out of valuables. It looked like there'd been a knockdown drag-out fight in the front room.

"What the fuck happened here?" Steele asked. "None of the others were torn apart."

"I'm wondering the same thing. Could it be different perps? Or maybe there was something else going on here."

"Do you still think Johnson is involved?"

"Yup. I do. There was something not right about him."

Steele nodded. They'd discussed their observations, and he'd agreed with Ethan after he'd met him. But if he was involved, why kill him? Did he want out? Maybe he got scared they were going to be caught or too greedy, and the rest of the group took him out. For now, they had a lot more questions and a lot fewer answers.

They were still going through the house when Ethan's phone rang. He expected it to be Anna. Instead, it was the uniform he'd sent to her house.

"Sir, I think you need to get over here. The garage door is up, and the car is in there, and the door to the house is open. There's no sign of Ms. Taggart but her keys and purse are on the garage floor, and there's blood."

"Damn. Don't touch anything."

"No, sir."

"Stay there, and don't let anyone in or out until we get there."

"No problem."

"What happened?" Steele asked concern etched on his face.

"It looks like someone grabbed Anna. C'mon we need to get over there. You call CSU, and I'll grab the LT away from the press."

Steele didn't bother to reply just pulled out his phone and started dialing. When they arrived at Anna's house, CSU was already there, and the uniform was standing guard. They ducked under the yellow crime scene tape, and he fired questions at the crime technician. "What have you got?"

The tech looked up at Ethan and shrugged. "Not a hell of a lot. We took samples of the blood and some mud we found on the floor, but there's not much else here. The place is clean. It looks like she was surprised by the way everything is on the floor."

"Do you think they killed her?" Ethan didn't want to say the words out loud, but he had to know. He wasn't the expert, but the tech in front of him was.

"No, I'd say there's a good chance she's alive. Not enough blood for a major injury. If I had to guess, I'd say she was knocked on the head."

He and Steele exchanged glances. They'd just come from another crime scene with a similar MO. It looked like Ethan's theory was proving itself.

CHAPTER TEN

Darkness. And pain. Deep throbbing pain. Unable to see, she tried to move, but she was tied to something. Even the littlest movement triggered a wave of nausea. She struggled to hold back the saliva and gagging. *Where the hell was she?* She tried to think, but it made her head hurt. Shit. Someone had been at her house, and she'd let them in when she opened the garage door. That had to be it. But where was she now? She probably only had two options. Don't move and pretend she was still unconscious or call out and hope someone would come to her rescue before whoever took her came back. Unless they were still there and watching her. Fear raced down her spine followed by another wave of nausea. She was well and truly screwed.

"I know you're awake, bitch."

Okay, that answered that question. Obviously hostile. *Think, Anna. What did your class teach you—figure out your surroundings.* Taking a deep breath, she tried to calm her racing heart. She'd get out of this, Ethan would find her, right? Except he'd told her to stay home and probably didn't even realize she was missing. It was anyone's guess how long he'd be stuck at the crime scene. It could be tomorrow before he got back and realized she was gone.

She was on her own. It's okay, she had the skills. At least that's what the certificate hanging in her office said. She'd already figured out that her arms were tied together by rope—not handcuffs—which was much better. There had to be a blindfold around her eyes, that would have been easier than making sure the whole room was dark. If she couldn't see, she couldn't identify them, so maybe they weren't planning on killing her. A spark of hope ignited. She just needed to keep fanning the flames and figure out how to get the hell out of there.

"I'm talking to you, bitch. What, you think you're too good to talk to me?" Without any warning, something hit her hard on the side of her face. After the intense pain and wooziness had subsided, she realized he'd punched her. Nice.

"Way to go. Oooh, a macho man. Hitting a woman who's tied up and helpless. I'm so scared." Either she was crazy, incredibly brave, or a little of both. She wasn't sure. But she'd rather be killed fast rather than deal with slow painful torture if that was his intention.

The room smelled weird, something she'd encountered before but she couldn't place it. It had to be a large open space from the way his voice echoed. Then she heard another voice. "You really shouldn't antagonize him. It's a good way to end up dead."

That voice she recognized, she should, she'd heard it often enough. It had to be a mistake. Had she been forced into it? There's no way she would have done this on her own, would she? Either that or Anna really was a terrible judge of character.

"She's right. But I'd love to teach you a lesson or two. Fucking stuck up bitch. Think you know everything. Well, we showed her, didn't we, girl?"

Another clue. *They knew each other? Was it Mr. Creepy Pants who'd taken her?*

"Yup, we did. And I'd say she had no idea. Probably thought they were pulling a fast one and we didn't know what she and her boyfriend were up to."

"What do you want? Why am I here?" Anna hoped if she got them talking maybe she'd be able to figure out an escape plan, or something, *anything,* to help her get out of there before it got worse.

"You haven't figured it out yet?"

"No. Why don't you tell me?"

Laughter, harsh, and scary echoed all around her. The throbbing in her head got worse. She probably had a concussion, but she doubted that would be what killed her. The more they spoke, the less hope she had about getting out of there alive.

"You think this is TV? The bad guys spilling their guts thinking they've already won. Nope. Sorry, bitch. If you can't figure it out, we're not going to help you."

"Why did you kill Hugh?"

The sound of a cigarette being stamped out was all she heard for a bit. Just when she figured they wouldn't answer her, he started talking again. Maybe he wasn't as smart as he thought he was. She was good at this game. She'd gotten Steele to come clean, and he was a trained professional. If this was Mr. Creepy Pants, there's no way he was a professional anything. Other than a hired killer maybe.

"Hugh was a piece of shit and my brother. He thought he was in charge, but I showed him. Stupid fuck. Ran up thousands of dollars in gambling debt and needed a way to pay the loan sharks."

Okay, well that made some sense anyway. Poor Betty.

"After your fuckin' boyfriend showed up he got worried. Tried to pull the plug. I told him he was a fucking pussy and that I'd run things from now on. He didn't like that idea so oops, night, night, Hugh."

"I didn't even know he had a brother. How could you kill your own blood?"

"We didn't grow up together. Our whore of a mother put us up for adoption. I didn't even track the fucker down 'til a couple of years ago."

It looked like getting him to talk wasn't going to be that difficult after all. If she could keep it up, maybe she could get her hands free. From the echo, she knew he wasn't close, and hopefully, he wouldn't be able to see her working on the knot. But then she'd forgotten about the other one, and that betrayal cut her to the core.

"Dad, you need to shut the hell up."

Dad? Dad? No wonder. But did he force her or was she a willing participant?

"It won't matter; by the time they find her, she'll be rat food."

Ugh really? Rat food? She hated rodents, their creepy little faces, and sharp teeth. Fear bubbled up inside her. *Calm down. Deep breaths. One. Two. Three. One...*

***

Ethan and Steele went inside and saw Anna's note about going to Betty Johnson's house. Obviously, she hadn't made it out of the garage on her own, but did Betty know anything?

With her note with the address in his hand, they headed to Betty Johnson's house. It was their best lead right now, and he needed to find Anna while she was still alive.

"It'll be okay. We'll find her," Steele said from the passenger side as he hung on to the suicide handles. Ethan didn't care if he broke every traffic law in the state, he wasn't going to waste one minute.

"Hell yeah, we will."

"Just remember, you're about to charge in to the house of an old woman who just found out her husband was murdered. We have no proof she was involved at all. We don't have proof he was either. Nothing turned up in the call logs."

"I know. I've got this."

"That's what I'm afraid of."

Ethan leveled a stare on Steele and the way the man blanched he was sure he looked as evil as he felt. Someone had his woman, and he was going to get her back, and God help anyone who stood in his way.

The lights were on at the Johnson's house, and there was already a patrol car parked outside. The front door was open, and Ethan walked in with Steele following. The white-haired old woman was sitting on the sofa, with a uniform next to her. She looked frail. And innocent. But time would tell. Ethan was done playing these games.

"Mrs. Johnson?"

The woman looked up, tears welling in her eyes and his heart softened just a little. Tears. Fuck. "Yes. Who are you?"

"I'm Detective Price, and this is my partner, Detective Brennan. Is it okay if we ask you a few questions?"

She nodded, and the uniformed officer got up and left the room.

"We're really sorry for your loss."

"Thank you. He wasn't much, but I loved him. For over fifty years, too." Ethan had a flash forward wondering if that's how he and Anna would be in fifty years. But not if he didn't find her.

"Did he have any enemies? Do you know why anyone would want to hurt him?"

"Oh, lots of people hated my Hugh, but they didn't really know him. At least until his good for nothing brother showed up."

Steele and Ethan exchanged looks. Now they were getting somewhere. "Who is his brother? We didn't show a brother in his records."

"They were separated when their mother put them up for adoption. Joe found Hugh a few months ago. I'm not sure how. That's when everything went to hell in a handbasket. Joe was just bad news."

"Do you know where Joe lives?"

"No, I'm sorry. He wouldn't come around often because he knew I didn't like him." Damn, so much for progress. Looked like another dead end.

"That's okay. I'm going to leave my card on the table here. If you think of anything, give us a call. We think he kidnapped Hugh's boss, and we need to find her before she gets hurt too."

"Oh no? Not Miss Taggart? What a lovely woman. Why would...oh never mind. He's a bad egg. I know he was working at the lumber yard off Heritage, but I think they fired him a couple of months ago."

"Thank you, Mrs. Johnson. And again, we're very sorry for your loss."

Ethan couldn't get out of there fast enough. He had a destination now, and if his gut was right, he was about to rescue a damsel in distress.

Steele called the LT and told him where they were heading. Ethan knew the lumber yard and gauged it would take him about ten minutes, five if he really pushed it. He really pushed it. Steele mumbled the entire time about lunatics behind the wheel as he clung to the suicide handle for dear life. Ethan didn't know what he was talking about, he was totally in control, even if he'd only barely missed the eighteen-wheeler on his last turn.

He wanted to arrive with his siren blaring, but he knew better. They had no idea how unstable Joe Johnson was or who else with him. He still believed it was a whole crew that worked the burglaries. He should find out soon enough if he was right.

Lights off as he turned into the parking lot, he practically coasted up to the front of the building. It looked locked up, but on the second floor, there was a dim light shining through one of the windows. Carefully getting out of the car, and pushing the door shut, he walked over to his lieutenant who was already there. How he'd arrived so fast, Ethan had no idea, but he didn't care either. He was going in to save Anna with or without his boss' approval.

"What do we know?"

"Not much. I ran Joseph Johnson and came up empty, but you said he was adopted, right?

"Yeah."

"He probably has a different last name. The panel van used in the robberies is parked around back, and so is a car and the green pickup truck Anna saw. I'd say we have our man, or crew, however, it turns out."

"I'm going in," Ethan said as he turned toward the building.

"Whoa, hold up there, cowboy. You need a plan, and you're not going in alone. You'll have backup."

"Fine. What's the plan?"

"I have Simmons and Mercier heading around the back to cover the exit, you and Steele go in the front, and the rest of us will be on standby for whoever needs us. Use the radio only if you need assistance. We don't want to let them know we're out here."

"Right."

"Good luck, Ethan. Steele, don't let him do anything stupid."

"Yeah, right! Like I could stop him."

As they approached the front, Steele pointed to the metal stairs on the outside of the building. It was a risk. They might creak, or come crashing down from their weight, but it definitely seemed like the best option to the second floor—and the quickest.

Ethan went first, carefully taking a step at a time. They seemed solid and, so far, no noise. As he climbed the stairs, he whispered, "Please God, let Anna be okay. I can't live without her now that I've found her."

A hand rested on his back, and he almost pulled his gun, before he realized Steele had caught up to him. Giving him the thumbs up, they continued climbing. Finally, they were on the second floor, the window was ajar, and he almost cheered. Voices. Anna's, a man who had to be Joe, and another woman. Fuck, no.

Ethan peered around the side of the window, hoping they weren't near enough to see him. He'd couldn't believe it. As the kids said, "mind blown." What the fuck was Jenny doing involved with this shit? She was practically still a kid.

Backing away, he whispered to Steele, "Two perps, Joe and Jenny. Anna's tied to a chair, but I didn't see anyone else. She looks a little banged up but okay."

"Jenny the receptionist? No fuckin' way. Are you sure?"

"I wish I wasn't. So how do you want to do this?"

"Did you see any guns?"

"No. I say let's go through the window and charge them. Two of us, two of them."

Steele nodded. "On three?"

"Yup."

Then all hell broke loose. He and Steele pushed the window open and charged in guns drawn, at almost the same time Mercier and Simmons hit the back stairs. His radio lit up, "shots fired, shots fired." Ethan didn't stop. The others could take care of the rest of the crew, he was going for Johnson or whatever his name was. Slamming into the dirtbag and knocking him down gave him a certain satisfaction. But mostly he didn't want to give him a chance to pull a gun.

But he hadn't anticipated the knife. Joe's blade slid between his ribs, but it didn't stop Ethan. Backing up, he shot him in the arm, even though killing the asshole would have been more satisfying. He glanced over and saw Jenny handcuffed and sitting on the floor. He wanted to be the one to interrogate her and find out why the fuck she'd turned on Anna.

Racing over to Anna, he ripped the bloody blindfold from her head and smiled into her startled eyes. "Your knight is here to rescue you."

"Ethan!" Tears rolled down her cheeks, leaving trails in the blood and dirt.

"Are you okay? Did he hurt you?"

"No, I mean I'm okay. I might have a concussion, and my face hurts where he punched me. But I'm okay."

"Thank God. I've never been so worried in my life."

"Me either. Oh my God, you're bleeding."

"I'm fine. It's merely a flesh wound." Then turning to Steele, he yelled, "Toss me that knife, I can't get these ropes untied." He never heard Steele's response or caught the knife. He'd fallen to the floor unconscious.

EPILOGUE

The sound of beeping woke him. Bright. Fuck. Where the hell was he? Then the harsh antiseptic hospital scent permeated his foggy brain. For a minute, he thought he was back in Iraq until his eyes focused on Anna. She was sitting in a chair beside the bed.

"Good morning. How's my hero?"

"Morning? How long have I been out?"

"A little over a day. Kind of. Depending on how you count it. You needed surgery. Apparently, the knife sliced through something important, and you almost died on me."

"I'm sorry I didn't mean to."

"You're on R&R for a while. No chasing bad guys for at least eight weeks. At least, I think that's what the doctor said."

"You scared the shit out of me. When the uniform told me there was blood at your house, I'd thought I lost you for good. I had to save you."

"I'd been praying for you to find me. I swear I thought I was dead for sure. You'd told me to stay home and didn't even know I was out. I'm surprised you found me so fast."

"Me too. Thank God you left that note about going to Betty's. She knew all about Hugh's brother, and that's how we found you."

"I told you she was a wonderful woman, not at all like Hugh. I'm going to have to help her out. I feel so bad for her."

"Help her out how?"

"I don't know. I'll figure something out. Maybe set her up in a senior community. Someplace where she can start over and have a nice place her kids can visit."

"You'd do that for her? Her husband almost got you killed."

"Yes, I would, and it was her husband who was bad not Betty."

"You're amazing, you were almost killed, and you're worrying about her. Are you okay? Did he hurt you? There was blood on the blindfold..."

"Yes, I'm fine. A concussion like I expected, but after I begged they let me stay here with you. The nurse would check on you and make sure I didn't fall asleep that first night, after that they didn't worry too much."

"Are you sure? No internal bleeding or anything?"

"No, Ethan. I'm fine, really. He didn't do much just smacked me a few times. You are the one who almost died. You promised to be careful."

"I was careful, and I didn't die, did I? I'm right here."

"Yes. You are. And we've all been waiting for you to wake up."

"All?"

"Yup, Steele's been keeping me company, and Adria." She nodded toward the corner of the room where the two of them were sitting together, whispering.

"Oh, and Steele might have let a certain cat out of the bag yesterday while we were waiting for you to get done with surgery."

"Cat, bag? What?"

"Yeah. Apparently, the ESP crew looked into my finances during the investigation. There were some questions about money I'd been taking out of my accounts. Why didn't you just ask me?"

Shit. Maybe he should have died on the operating table if she was going to break up with him now. If he'd had the strength, he would have gotten out of bed and killed Steele with his bare hands. "Did he also tell you it wasn't my idea?"

"Yes, he mentioned that, but again, why didn't you ask me about it?"

"There wasn't a good time, we were caught up in the investigation, and you were just starting to trust in us. I knew you weren't involved in anything bad."

"You did? You trusted me that much?"

"Yes, was I wrong to?"

"No. You weren't wrong. So, ask me."

"Ask you what?"

She sighed, and he was confused. Maybe the anesthesia hadn't worn all the way off. But at least she was still sitting there, she hadn't told him to screw off, hadn't left, wasn't even yelling. In fact, it looked like she was smiling. Maybe he was still drugged up.

"Ask me what the money is for."

"I don't care, it's your money."

"Ugh, sometimes, Ethan. If you hadn't just saved my life and almost lost yours. I might have to hurt you. The money is for Tag's new rehab facility and clinic. I've been taking the money out of various accounts to spread it around. So you see, nothing nefarious."

"I knew there wasn't, but thank you for not getting mad at me."

"I didn't say I wasn't mad, but after Steele explained it was all his idea, I understood. Besides, how could I be mad at you? You risked everything to save me."

"I was so worried. You have no idea."

"We'll work on it. I'm sorry I've made things more difficult than they should have been."

"It doesn't matter, baby. I love you. We'll figure it all out."

"Yes, we will."

"And Steele and Adria? I guess you've been matchmaking?"

"Who, me? What is it they say about people who are happy and in love? That they want to share it with the world, or something like that."

"Yeah, something like that. Does that mean you're happy and in love?"

"Actually, I've been meaning to let you in on a little secret. Ethan Price, you've swept me off my feet, and I'm totally cow jumped over the moon in love with you."

If you've enjoyed *A Soldier's Pledge*, I hope you'll take the time to leave a review. Look for *A Soldier's Redemption*, Tag and Julie's story, coming soon. Lynne xoxo

Lynne St. James

ABOUT THE AUTHOR

Lynne St. James is a member of the Romance Writers of America and has been writing for as long as she can remember. Her lifelong dream to be published came true in 2012 when her first book was released through Siren Publishing. That was just the beginning. Since then she's written four different series.

She lives in the in the mostly sunny state of Florida with her husband and a small petting zoo. Okay maybe it's not a zoo, but sometimes it feels like it. With an eighty-five-pound fluffy Dalmation-mutt horse-dog, a fourteen-pound Yorkie-poo, and two cats, she thinks it qualifies for zoo status. And though Lynne likes to pretend that her office is her private domain, you can usually find one or more of her furry babies keeping her company.

When Lynne's not writing, she's reading, taking pictures, and sometimes even cooking—to the great relief of her hubby. But mostly she's in her office with a huge mug of coffee surrounded by books, stuffed animals, and post-it notes while writing her next happily ever after.

Where to find Lynne:

Email: lynne@lynnestjames.com
Facebook: https://www.facebook.com/authorLynneStJames
Website: http://lynnestjames.com
VIP Newsletter sign-up: http://eepurl.com/bT99Fj

BOOKS BY LYNNE ST. JAMES

Beyond Valor
A Soldier's Gift, Book 1
A Soldier's Surprise, Book 2 – A Barefoot Bay Kindle World Novella
A Soldier's Triumph, Book 3 – ESP Agency Novel
Protecting Faith, Book 4 – A Special Forces: Operation Delta Kindle World Novella
A Soldier's Pledge, Book 5 –ESP Agency Novel
A Soldier's Redemption, Book 6 (Coming Soon)

Raining Chaos
Taming Chaos, Book 1
Seducing Wrath, Book 2
Music under the Mistletoe, Book 2.5 – A Raining Chaos Christmas (Novella)
Tempting Flame, Book 3

Anamchara
Embracing Her Desires, Book 1
Embracing Her Surrender, Book 2
Embracing Her Love, Book 3

Lynne St. James

The Vampires of Eternity
Twice Bitten Not Shy, Book 1
Twice Bitten to Paradise, Book 2
Twice Bitten and Bewitched, Book 3

Want to be one of the first to learn about Lynne St. James's new releases? Sign up for her VIP newsletter filled with exclusive news and contests but never spam! http://eepurl.com/bT99Fj

A Soldier's Gift – Beyond Valor 1

Can this wounded hero finally find love?

Lieutenant Thomas "Mac" MacDonald pulls three of his unit's soldiers from their burning Humvee when a roadside bomb explodes in Afghanistan. During the rescue, he sustains a severe head injury that leaves him believing he's dying—until he wakes up stateside alive but blind.

Beth's life changed forever with one phone call. An accident leaves her ex-husband and daughter fighting for their lives. Putting her life on hold, she spends most of her time in the hospital with her daughter, praying she'll pull through while her ex's condition goes downhill, forcing her to make one of the hardest decisions of her life.

Meeting Beth while volunteering at the hospital after his discharge, Mac is instantly attracted to her. As he struggles to come to grips with what life has dealt him, he finds his thoughts continuously turning to a woman he barely knows.

Despite all odds, these two wounded hearts begin to find a love they both need and deserve. But when Mac's secret comes to light will Beth be blinded by the past or embrace her destiny in Mac's arms?

What readers are saying about **A Soldier's Gift**:

"This book takes you on an amazing journey one of discovery, love, and life. I thought it was truly beautiful as well heart-wrenching especially the beginning of the book it had me in tears…" ~ Heidi, Cariad Book Reviews

"Awesome story I loved everything about this book. Very well written. I will definitely read more of Lynne's books. I can't wait." ~ Tina Sheridan

"I don't usually enjoy soldier books, but this one blew me away. I can't wait to read the rest of this series." ~ Jenny

A Soldier's Surprise – Beyond Valor 2
(A Barefoot Bay Kindle World Novella)

An anniversary celebration they'd never forget…in Barefoot Bay!

Chloe accepted that once again she'd be celebrating their anniversary alone while Logan was deployed in Afghanistan. She should be used to it, except she wasn't. It was their tenth, and she'd hoped somehow things would be different, especially when she finds out she's pregnant with their third child.

Logan's offered an assignment he can't pass up—and now he'll be able to surprise his wife for their anniversary. With a romantic weekend planned in Barefoot Bay, he can't wait to get home and see the look on Chloe's face.

After being whisked away to the exclusive Casa Blanca resort, Chloe wrestles with the decision whether or not to tell Logan about the baby. Struggling with the thought of raising another child by herself while he's in constant danger and thousands of miles away weighs on her heart. Will it be a welcome surprise or ruin their special weekend?

What readers are saying about ***A Soldier's Surprise***:

"I really enjoyed this book & it's a quick view of the military personnel & their families. As the reader, you are given a glimpse at what they have to go through in their lives & their struggles to defend. Would recommend this book to everyone." ~ PamD

"I usually don't read the military books as it is too close to reality for me and I would rather read more fantasy stuff, but this book really hooked me from the first page, and I couldn't stop reading." ~ Cheryl Bulone

"Loved this book. A wonderful love story about a soldier serving in Afghanistan who is able to take his wife of ten years on an Anniversary trip to the Florida Keys. A totally realistic heartwarming story that I couldn't put down until I finished the book. Be prepared to cry!" ~ Marilyn

A Soldier's Triumph – Beyond Valor 3
An Eagle Security & Protection Agency Novel

He'd make them pay for brutalizing his wife!

Wounded in action, Alex Barrett is stuck in a wheelchair. But it won't stop him from protecting the love of his life. Come hell or high water, he'd find a way to keep Lily safe.

Devastated at how close she came to losing her husband, Lily Barrett will do anything to protect him--even if it means not telling him when her life is in danger.

When Alex finds out, he enlists the help of some old teammates who run the Eagle Protection & Security Agency. Will these ex-military men be able to help Alex save his wife before it's too late?

What readers are saying about ***A Soldier's Triumph***:

"I found this story to be very good! The story was very vivid along with great dialogue. The story is suspenseful with mystery and romance. I highly recommend this book." ~ Julie Reads Books

"I loved this book! Ms. St. James entertained us with a moving story of an Army Ranger Alex, and his wife, Lily." ~ Julie Ann Francher

"Lynne St James has done it again! A great read from beginning to end. So good to read about characters I made a connection with in the first two books in the Eagle Security & Protection series. Lynne never fails to deliver the excitement, be it plot twists or the sexy bits that keep you reading late into the night." ~ Pamela Talley

Protecting Faith – Beyond Valor 4
An Eagle Security & Protection Agency Novel
(A Special Forces Kindle World Novella)

Will he be able to keep her safe?

After finishing a job in San Diego, Ex-SEAL Chase "Frost" Brennan stopped by to see old friends. Meeting up with Wolf and the rest of his team at their old hangout, the last person he expected to see was the only woman he'd ever loved and the only one he couldn't have. But maybe this was his second chance.

Faith Murdock was a civilian psychologist for the Navy by day and burlesque dancer by night. Dancing was her release. It kept her sane and helped her forget the one patient she couldn't help--a Navy SEAL who'd stolen her heart.

When she started receiving anonymous notes, she thought it was nothing. Then they became threatening, and she knew she had to ask for help.

There were only a few people she trusted, and Wolf and Caroline were two of them. The other was Frost, but that was a long time ago. Seeing him at her show was like a dream come true. But she still wondered if it was a coincidence or was he her stalker?

Faith wasn't the same woman he'd lost three years ago, and Frost had his work cut out for him. But with the help of Wolf's team, he'd do what it took to catch the stalker and save his woman. Because whether she knew it or not, she was his and this time she wasn't getting away.

What readers are saying about **Protecting Faith**:

"I love second chance at love stories and St. James really pulls this one off. Chase and Faith are the perfect couple. All the reasons why they couldn't be together no longer apply, and it's nice how this story comes together, and they get their HEA ending." ~ Vickie Chaisson

"Lynne St. James has written another amazing book. What two things in life go better together than Ms. St James in a Susan Stoker Kindle World. I loved every last page of this book and had to reread it just so I could hang onto Faith and Chase/Frost a little longer. Bravo Ms. St. James!" ~ JLP Gassman

"I love a happy ending for those who serve to protect us and our way of life. When a hardened warrior meets a strong willed, independent woman, you just know that sparks will fly. A great read with suspense and action keeping us turning pages until we reach the end." ~ Jean Ross

A Soldier's Pledge – Beyond Valor 5
(An Eagle Security & Protection Agency Novel)

He'd do anything to keep her safe...
Ethan Price thought a job as a small-town police detective in Willow Haven would be easy after five years as a pilot in the Air Force. Then a rash of break-ins put the entire department on alert and the woman he loves at risk.

Too stubborn for her own good...
Anna Taggart is smart, stubborn, independent, and doesn't think she needs anyone. Having her heart broken before, she refuses to give in to her feelings for Ethan no matter how hard he pursues her.

Can he get through to her before it's too late?
When the clues lead to someone close to Anna, Ethan has his work cut out for him. With help from his partner, Steele, and the team at Eagle Security & Protection he is determined to solve the case and keep Anna safe. But will Ethan be able to convince Anna that life is too short not to give in to love?

What reviewers and readers are saying about ***A Soldier's Pledge***:

"Reading a book by author Lynne St James is like eating a chocolate chip cookie- the characters are these delicious little chocolate chips intertwined with the cookie dough, making a truly rich and delicious treat for her readers." ~ California girl in MA

"Be prepared to be swept away in Anna and Ethan's story! The characters are real life and a perfect blend of Romance and danger! Loved this book!" ~ Christine E.

"I still ADORE Lynne St. James! Her books have the perfect balance of romance and suspense with plenty of heart and on the edge of your seat action. Soldier's Pledge is a delight! I LOOOOOVE Lynne's writing and this cover...just GORGEOUS! You won't be disappointed with this read!" ~ Marie's Temping Reads

Lynne St. James

A Soldier's Pledge

Made in the USA
Monee, IL
06 March 2020